Trouble for Angie

✳ ✳ ✳

With a groan Angie pushed herself back up onto the seat. No way she was going to come out of this whole thing looking like anything but a criminal, she thought unhappily, remembering how she'd smuggled the horror video back to Potter's under her shirt.

A horror video, the kind she was expressly forbidden to watch, let alone own, and paid for with stolen money. Well, maybe not stolen, exactly, but borrowed. Any way you looked at it, it was money that wasn't hers to spend.

✳ ✳ ✳

Angie the Airhead

Angie the Airhead

Mary Towne

Rainbow Bridge®

Troll Associates

Copyright © 1995 by Mary Spelman.

Cover illustration copyright © 1995 by Wayne Alfano.

Published by Troll Associates, Inc. Rainbow Bridge is a trademark of Troll Associates.

Printed in the United States of America.

10 9 8 7 6 5 4 3 2 1

Angie the Airhead

Chapter

✻ ✻ ✻

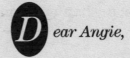 *ear Angie,*

I hope you're having a good time up in Vermont. It's really hot and boring here.

I'm writing because my mom saw a sale at Moore's on some green shorts with white stripes down the side, just like we've been wanting for the club. They're not real satin, I guess, but they're not sleaze, either. The only thing is, we have to get them now, while they still have enough for everyone, and I guess you took the money box up there with you, right?

Anyway, my mom's being a real pal for once and using her credit card. She says you can pay her back as soon as you get home.

Just don't lose the key. (Joke!)
See ya—

Your friend,
Courtney

Angie read the letter for the third time, hoping the words might have changed somehow. But of course they hadn't. With a sigh, she stuffed the sheet of notepaper back into the pocket of her shorts. Then she slid off the stern seat of the red canoe, wriggled under the center strut, and stretched out on the bottom, fitting her spine to the canoe's and draping her legs over the forward seat.

From this position—one most people would have found impossible to achieve in a canoe—all Angie could see was the blue summer sky. The middle of Heron Lake was her favorite place for getting away from bother and fuss and people reminding her of things she'd forgotten to do. Lying this way, letting the canoe drift while the water gurgled and lisped against its curving sides, Angie felt she might be looking into the depths of the universe—maybe even into the depths of her own soul. If it was empty and cloudless, as it was today, so much the better.

"Don't lose the key." Some joke. Angie only wished she had. Then there would still be $40.66 in the metal cashbox under her bed, instead of just $25.82.

Her family might think it was hilarious that Angie had been elected treasurer of anything, even a baton-twirling club with only seven members, but in fact Angie had a good head for figures. She knew to a penny what she'd borrowed from the box and would have to replace between now and a week from Sunday: $14.84.

Green shorts, she thought distractedly. But she was almost sure they'd decided on blue, with purple as a second choice. It was Courtney who'd wanted green, because of her eyes. Angie hoped it wouldn't be that yucky bright green like they used for St. Patrick's Day decorations, along with bright pink, double yuck. Those were the colors she always used to get stuck with for her birthday parties, because of being born in the middle of March. A little later and she could have had Easter colors—a lighter green, plus yellow and lavender instead of pink.

Angie blinked, willing herself to see only the deep, soothing blue of the sky over Heron Lake. Still, a birthday party was a happy, fun kind of thing to be thinking about, even a noisy little kids' birthday party in the wrong colors. It was certainly more fun than thinking about asking her parents for an advance on her September allowance and then explaining why she needed it.

"Oh, Angie," her mother would say, shaking her head. "You mean you've run through your August allowance already?"

If her brother Steve was around, he'd laugh and say

11

she'd run through it the first week she had it. He knew, because she'd had to borrow a dollar fifty from him for the jumbo bag of popcorn she always bought for the long drive from Connecticut up to Potter's Lodge.

Even if she deleted Steve from the scene, her father was bound to ask what there was to spend money on around here anyway. "Surely you can't have run up a fourteen-dollar tab for Cokes this soon," he'd say, referring to the old soda chest on the back porch of the lodge. Nora and Ray ran it on an honor system—you helped yourself and signed your name on a sheet of paper tacked to the wall above it.

Angie would have to remind him of the shopping trip she'd made with her mother and her Aunt Marge last week over the border in Canada. "But I gave you money for the things you needed at the drugstore," her mother would point out. "Shampoo and a hairbrush because you forgot to pack them, and that pimple cream you don't even need." (It was true that Angie's skin was as clear and tanned this summer as it had ever been. Still, some of her friends at home were getting pimples, and she figured it was just as well to be prepared.) "You mean you bought something else?"

"With what?" Steve would put in. Except he wasn't going to be part of this conversation, Angie reminded herself hastily. That meant she wouldn't have to confess that she'd helped herself to fifteen dollars from the club cashbox just in case she saw anything she wanted to buy.

Well, she would explain, of course, but maybe not right away. And when she did, she'd also explain that she'd thought she'd have plenty of time to pay the money back before the club's first meeting, after school started.

Meanwhile, though, her parents would still be waiting to hear where the $14.84 had gone, and Angie would have to say that while her mother and Aunt Marge were trying on cashmere sweaters in the fancy woolens shop they visited every year, she'd seen this little video store around the corner—

"A video?" her father would demand. "What kind of video?"

With a groan Angie pushed herself back up onto the stern seat, causing the imaginary scene to shatter and dissolve like the reflection of the canoe in the water. No way she was going to come out of this whole thing looking like anything but a criminal, she thought unhappily, remembering how she'd smuggled the horror video back to Potter's under her shirt. In fact, now that she thought of it, that really *was* criminal, since she hadn't declared the video at Customs when they recrossed the border to Vermont. Then she'd hidden it under a loose floorboard in her room.

A horror video, the kind she was expressly forbidden to watch, let alone own, and paid for with stolen money. Well, maybe not stolen, exactly, but borrowed. Any way you looked at it, it was money that wasn't hers to spend.

Chapter

✳ ✳ ✳

H ello there, Angie," called a pleasant voice over a faint creaking of oarlocks.

Angie looked up to see Mrs. Rowan sculling a rowboat in the direction of the dock, wearing her familiar battered khaki hat and a pair of binoculars slung around her neck. She hadn't realized there was anyone else out on the lake. Mrs. Rowan must have been bird-watching over by the far shore, which was still in deep green shadow in late morning.

"Such a long face on this beautiful day! Aren't you feeling well? I know there's a nasty summer cold going around."

"Oh, I'm fine," Angie assured her, quickly turning up the corners of her mouth in a smile. When Mrs. Rowan shipped her oars and continued to look at her quizzically, she added, "I guess I must just be getting hungry."

"Yes, I'm heading back in for lunch myself."

Back to her cabin, she meant. Mrs. Rowan rarely had breakfast or lunch in the lodge dining room, since as a niece of the late Ephraim Potter, the founder of Potter's Lodge and Family Camp, she owned her own fully equipped cabin, with a real kitchen instead of just the kitchenette that came with some of the guest cabins.

"If you're looking for someone to picnic with," Mrs. Rowan added, "I think Rita's up on the Ledge Trail. She was going to practice her wind sprints there. Something to do with altitude and gradients." She sighed. "Of course, she's used to being a mile high, back home in Colorado."

"Oh, I brought my sandwiches with me," Angie said hastily, realizing in the same moment that she hadn't. Drat it, she'd left her lunch back in Cedar Waxwing. (All the cabins had been named by Mrs. Rowan after birds—all except her own, come to think of it. Maybe she'd run out of names.) She scrambled forward and picked up her paddle, hoping Mrs. Rowan wouldn't notice the absence of a lunch sack at the bottom of the canoe. Mrs. Rowan was always trying to get kids to pal around with her visiting granddaughter, Rita Crawford. So far the only person who had was Wanda Munson, whom Angie considered a special case, almost as baffling as Rita herself.

"Well, if you see Rita, tell her I have some chores for

her back at the cabin. Beth didn't show up this morning—I expect she's down with that cold—and the bathroom could use a good scrubbing, now Rita's finally gotten her crayfish out of there." Mrs. Rowan made a wry face, and Angie nodded. Rita was always saving or collecting something weird. "Beth refused to clean it, and I can't say I blame her."

Beth was one of the chambermaids, a local girl whose boyfriend rode her in to the lodge on his motorcycle each morning, obeying the posted fifteen-mile-an-hour speed limit but raising a great cloud of dust and scaring all the birds away. No one expected Beth to walk all the way in from the state highway, but people thought she could at least have asked to be dropped off at the head of the lake, where the dirt road turned into Potter's driveway.

But Nora said staff was hard to come by in this remote northeastern part of Vermont, and she wasn't about to rock the boat—or, in this case, the motorcycle. She left it to her husband Ray to do the apologizing, something he was good at. Angie's Uncle Maury was fond of pointing out that as managers, the Wallaces had arrived at an efficient division of labor: Nora kept the machinery propped up and in running order, and Ray supplied the oil.

As Mrs. Rowan pulled away toward the dock, Angie found herself wondering how much the maids got paid for dusting and sweeping and cleaning bathrooms.

Probably not very much, since Potter's couldn't afford to pay anybody very much. It was owned by a private corporation that always seemed to be on the brink of financial collapse. Each spring there were urgent phone calls among the stockholders—who included Angie's parents, her aunt and uncle, and several of the other longtime guests—to see if the place was really going to be able to open again for the summer.

On the other hand, the maids didn't do all that great a job, Angie thought—hardly any better than she herself did when her mother made her clean up her room at home. Not that anyone cared, since Potter's was sort of casual and shabby and untidy, in a nice kind of way. If you minded things like spiderwebs at the back of your closet or dust between the floorboards— supposing the floorboards even met closely enough to hold dust—Potter's was not the place to come on your vacation.

Angie had dipped her paddle into the water. Now she brought it up again and sat gazing absently at the distant tennis court to the right of the dock. Someone was hitting against the new backboard Ray had installed. Whoever it was wasn't very good. Each thud of the ball against the boards was followed by a long pause, as if the person had missed and was having to chase the ball into a far corner.

Angie blinked. What was it she'd been thinking about? Oh, yes, the maids and the money they earned.

And before that, about the money she herself needed to get. Slowly she put the two thoughts together. What if—?

But no, her parents would never let her work as a chambermaid, not even temporarily while Beth was out sick; not even if Nora and Ray would hire her, which Angie was pretty sure they wouldn't. This wasn't just because she was too young, besides being a guest, but also because of the time last summer her parents had made her volunteer for the cleanup squad after a lobster cookout over at the big lake. Not only had Angie neglected to swab off the picnic table she'd been assigned (well, it looked like it might rain, and besides the lake water was so cold), she'd forgotten to bring back the garbage bag she'd also been assigned. Because of the smell and the ants and other things Angie didn't even want to think about, the whole swimming area had had to be declared off limits the next day.

Angie wrinkled her nose at the memory. How had she gotten thinking about *that*, of all gross things? Oh, yes, because of needing to earn money. Well, okay, maybe she couldn't do cleaning, but there must be other kinds of work she could do here at Potter's. Even people on vacation must have errands that needed running, she thought vaguely, or odd jobs they'd just as soon pay someone else to do. Angie wasn't sure just what these things might be, but once she started looking for them, she was bound to spot quite a few. And even if no one paid her very much at a time, how long could it take to earn the measly sum of $14.84?

Feeling energized now that she had a plan of action—even if it wasn't a very definite one—and also suddenly ravenous for her peanut butter sandwiches and spice cookies, Angie dug her paddle into the water and sped toward the dock. She was halfway there when a small, white-clad figure appeared around the corner of the tennis court fence and began picking its way gingerly along the reed-fringed bank below it. This could only be one person: Hugh Curtis, who must have hit his ball over the fence.

Angie braked the canoe to what would have been a skidding halt if she'd been riding a bike. She should have known it was Hugh on the tennis court, just from the sound of the ball against the backboard—or rather the lack of sound. For every ten swings Hugh took with his oversized racket, he was lucky if he connected twice. Being Hugh, he always wore his good tennis clothes even when there was no one around who'd play with him. And being Hugh, he also never thought to bring more than one ball.

Stealthily, before Hugh could look up and see her and ask her to help him find his ball, Angie turned the canoe toward shore and paddled swiftly into the shelter of some overhanging bushes. Ordinarily she wouldn't have minded helping, but Hugh was such a jumpy, distracting sort of kid, sort of like a grasshopper that might shoot off at any moment and hit you in the eye.

And right now Angie needed to concentrate.

Not that she could start on her project of earning money just yet—lunch would have to come first. Still, Angie knew herself well enough to realize that if she got involved in doing other stuff, even just stuff like looking for someone's tennis ball, she'd be in danger of letting the whole thing just sort of slide. Before she knew it, she'd be thinking about hitting against the backboard herself after lunch, and after that she'd want a swim to cool off. She'd get talking to Sally or someone over at the big lake, and pretty soon it would be time for a Coke back on the lodge veranda, followed by a game of badminton with Steve, if he was around, or Wanda if he wasn't. In the late afternoon, she'd ride her bike up to Marie's store on the state highway to see the new kittens in the back storeroom, and maybe get an ice-cream bar or a bag of chips to eat on the ride back. . . .

Except she didn't have the money for ice cream or chips, Angie reminded herself. This wasn't really a problem, since she could always charge at Marie's—her parents would grumble but pay. Still, it just went to show. If she wasn't careful, the days would go by in the usual pleasant Potter's haze, and then suddenly she'd be back in Connecticut, and Courtney's mother would be holding out her hand for the $40.66 that Angie's own treasurer's report said should be in the club cashbox.

With a sigh, Angie paddled up along the shoreline toward a muddy stretch of bank where she could beach the canoe while she went up and got her lunch from the cabin. You weren't supposed to leave a canoe unattended like that, not since the time Sally North had gone ashore up by the beaver dam to read under a shady tree and looked up an hour later to find her canoe drifting around by itself out in the middle of the lake. But Angie promised herself she'd be quick. Anyway, the only person who'd tell on her was her brother Steve, and he was up behind the car shed, helping Hal, the part-time handyman, split logs for kindling.

Steve was weird that way, Angie thought, nosing the canoe around a sunken log—he actually liked working. Of course, he also liked to have everyone *notice* him working. Angie frowned as it occurred to her that having people notice her working was just what she couldn't afford, assuming she could find any work to do in the first place. It would be too out of character, and people—her family especially—would be bound to start asking questions. And if there was one thing Angie knew for sure, it was that there weren't going to be any satisfactory answers to the question of why she needed $14.84.

Chapter

* * *

Early that afternoon, wearing a pair of laceless old sneakers, her faded blue bathing suit, and a towel slung around her shoulders, Angie sauntered along the trail to Great Harriman Lake, pretending to have nothing more on her mind than going for a swim. Since this was pretty much what she was apt to be doing on any hot, sunny afternoon at Potter's, the pretense didn't require a whole lot of effort. The effort lay in remembering that she wasn't *just* going for a swim. She also had a plan.

Angie had tacked this plan up in large letters in what she thought of as the front of her mind and numbered its parts like a homework assignment:

    1) Teach someone to swim.

    2) Be a lifeguard for someone who doesn't
       know how to swim.

3) Be a baby-sitter.

In capitals at the bottom, she'd added: DO NOT ASK FOR MONEY. This was important because, as she'd realized earlier, if she went around asking for paying jobs, people might want to know what she needed the money for. Instead, she'd just have to wait and hope they'd tip her. She wouldn't actually hold out her hand, she decided, only stand still and look sort of expectant. This was what the high-school boy at home did when he delivered groceries from the fancy market in town. When her mother finally noticed him still standing in the kitchen doorway, she'd give him an apologetic smile and rummage in her purse for a dollar or two.

As the trail widened into a vista of glittering blue water with a few white sails in the distance, it occurred to Angie that people over at the swimming area probably wouldn't have purses or wallets with them. She might have to go hang around them later and hope they'd notice her and remember. Except tonight was square-dance night at the rec house, and how could you hang around people who were square dancing? You wouldn't get noticed, you'd only get stepped on.

Angie shook her head. She was starting to act like Wanda Munson, worrying about a whole bunch of stuff that hadn't even happened yet. One thing at a time, she told herself firmly. And the first thing was to do a job for someone.

She came to the grassy picnic area, bounded on the

left by the boathouse annex and on the right by the big stone fireplace and the beginning of the Ledge Trail. Usually this was the point where Angie dropped her towel, kicked off her sneakers, and did a running dive into the lake from one of the flat granite rocks that served as a waterfront for Potter's half-mile stretch of shoreline. Great Harriman Lake was about twenty times bigger than Heron Lake and about twenty times colder. If you thought too long about going in, you never would.

Today, though, she made herself stop beside one of the picnic tables so she could see who was around and what the possibilities might be. As she'd figured, there were quite a few people here on this warm afternoon, some of them sunning themselves on the rocks, some of them splashing around inside the swimming area that was marked off by ropes attached to bleach-bottle floats. As usual, too, the raft had been taken over by a small group of older teenagers, including the three college girls who worked as waitresses in the dining room.

Angie dismissed the teenagers—they already knew how to swim, didn't need a lifeguard, and had no children—and edged over to the fireplace for a better look at the small triangle of beach where the young mothers and little kids usually hung out.

"Angie?" A familiar straw hat swiveled in her direction from one of the slant-back wooden armchairs facing the water below the picnic area. Angie frowned; she'd forgotten her mother and her Aunt Marge would probably be over here too. "Why are you lurking around up there? I thought you'd gone on the picnic to Dark Pool."

Only now did Angie remember she'd signed up for a picnic hike today, the one announced two days ago on the outdoor blackboard where Ray scribbled notes about upcoming activities. That must be where the others were—her cousin Gus, and Sally, and probably Steve, too. While she was eating her sandwiches in the canoe, she'd heard the pickup truck go rattling by on the dirt road but had thought nothing of it. And she *loved* going to Dark Pool, a circle of gleaming black water deep in the woods, where there was a little waterfall and a high rock from which you could jump or dive and never hit bottom.

Angie thought mournfully that at least this proved she was taking her money problem seriously. She didn't usually forget about things she liked, only about stuff she didn't want to do.

"Such a face!" Mrs. Hyatt said, taking off her dark glasses in order to study her daughter more closely. "Really, Angie, you look as if you'd lost your best friend."

Angie stopped herself from saying that she might be about to lose her six best friends—well, five, if she subtracted Kelly Miles, who thought she was cool enough to twirl two batons at once and who was always braining people with the baton she couldn't quite catch.

"Now, now," Aunt Marge chided her sister from the adjoining chair—though she, too, looked at Angie curiously. "Everyone's entitled to a down mood once in a while. And Angie's growing up, you know."

"You mean she's about to turn all sulky and *adolescent* on us? I can't stand it!" Angie's mother said with a groan. "It's bad enough having Steve telling me every half hour how to run my life. Do you know what he said to me this morning when I was going for my third cup of coffee?"

Though Angie would have liked to know what it was—probably something about taking a thermos to breakfast to save the extra trip, never mind that it was chatting with people on the veranda her mother cared about, not coffee—she seized her chance to escape down the little path to the beach.

What was all this about her face, anyway? Was having a secret problem making her look *different* somehow? Angie was pretty enough never to have spent a lot of time studying her appearance. Whenever she looked into a mirror, she saw more or less what she expected to see: a cloud of silky light hair framing a fine-boned face with large blue eyes, a short, straight nose, and a curving mouth that always seemed to be smiling a little.

Angie had vaguely assumed that the smile was a

27

permanent part of her expression, but of course it probably disappeared when she was mad or in trouble. And that was okay, she thought confusedly, because usually everyone *knew* when she was mad or in trouble. The tricky thing was having a private trouble instead of the usual public one. She realized she was going to have to do a lot of pretending, including smiling when she didn't feel like it. Angie was good at pretending to be somebody else—she loved acting— but she'd never before tried pretending to be herself.

Chapter

✳ ✳ ✳

S uppressing a sigh at this fresh complication, Angie laid her towel over a sumac bush, stepped out of her sneakers, and waded into the water to begin earning her way out of trouble.

Her target was a small boy she'd noticed earlier because of the way he kept dog-paddling in circles and then flopping forward to float face down for seconds at a time. When he ran out of breath—Angie could feel him beginning to tense and quiver—he'd raise his head with a gasp and start dog-paddling again.

This was definitely a kid who needed a swimming lesson, Angie decided. Unfortunately, as she got closer, she saw that it was also Andrew Munson, Wanda's little brother, a person no one could teach anything to. Angie herself had a short attention span, but Andrew's could be measured in eye blinks—if you could even get his attention in the first place. Still, she felt she had to try.

"Hi, Andrew," she said brightly. "Would you like me to give you a swimming lesson?"

Andrew had just come up for air again. He shook his head. "I already know how," he told her, and resumed his dog paddle.

Angie backed away to avoid being splashed, then decided she might as well get wet all over. Just ten yards from shore, the water was so cold that her bottom and legs were already numb, making her feel as if she'd been sawed in two. She dunked, wrung the water out of her hair, and said to Andrew, "I mean real swimming, when you lie down flat and move your arms out of the water."

When Andrew looked at her blankly, she demonstrated with a few strokes of her own swift crawl, then turned and swam back to him. "Like that."

Andrew shook his head. "I'm practicing to be a loon," he said. "And loons don't have arms."

Angie stared at him. "Right," she said finally.

"The hard part is holding my breath," Andrew continued. "Did you know a loon can hold his breath for a whole minute at a time? Maybe even more than that. They're not like a fish, see, that can breathe down in the water. They're like people that have to breathe in air. Except loons are birds—well, I guess everyone knows that. Anyway—"

"Loons dive," Angie interrupted a little wildly. She'd

forgotten the main reason Andrew had such a short attention span was that he also had a one-track mind.

"Well, sure," Andrew said, looking offended. "I didn't get to that part yet. They can fly and dive both. And—"

"So if you want to be a loon, you need to learn how to dive. Look, I'll show you."

The water was too shallow here, so Angie swam out where it was deeper, filled her lungs with air, and folded herself over into a neat surface dive, remembering to straighten her legs and point her toes as she thrust for the bottom.

She surfaced, blowing out her breath, and turned to give Andrew an encouraging smile, hoping he wouldn't start talking about loons not having long legs, either.

But he was shaking his head again. "That's too hard," he said as she swam back to him. "I might get scared and drown."

"Andrew, I wouldn't *let* you drown," Angie said in exasperation. "What kind of person do you think I am, anyway? All I want to do is give you a lesson."

Andrew considered this, tucking his hands beneath his armpits and sticking out his solid brown stomach. "Usually you're nice," he conceded, "but you might just be trying to duck me. Anyway, my mom doesn't like me to have lessons, because I forget things too fast. And anyway, I'm cold."

He turned and splashed back to shore. Angie saw Mrs. Munson sitting on a folding chair in the shady back corner where the tumble of rocks that served as a breakwater met the beach. She was plump and placid, like Andrew, though not nearly as tan. As she set her magazine aside and held out a towel for him, she gave Angie a warm smile—as if, Angie thought crossly, she'd just been being *nice* to Andrew.

There were three other mothers on the beach, all keeping an eye on their kids. So nobody needed a baby-sitter, Angie thought glumly, let alone a lifeguard. Then, looking at the youngest of the mothers—a tired-looking woman who was staying with her three children in Tree Swallow, the smallest of the cabins—Angie had an idea.

"Do you want to go for a swim?" she offered, stepping around the two-year-old, who was squatting in the sand with a wooden bucket and shovel. "I could watch the kids for you."

"Oh, would you?"

A moment ago, the woman had looked out for the count, flattened against her low beach chair like something washed up after a storm. Now she sprang to her feet, said, "Just don't let Miranda throw sand on the baby," and plunged into the lake.

Angie looked around for the baby and found it lying in a basket wedged back among the reeds that fringed the base of the rock ledge—a little like Moses in the bulrushes, she thought, except Moses probably hadn't been wearing a white sunhat with yellow smiley-faces on it.

"And Jonathan can't go in the water because he has a cold," the mother called over her shoulder. She was already halfway to the raft. Angie nodded, and the mother swam away with long, powerful strokes. Angie didn't see her again for twenty minutes.

It was a long twenty minutes. Twice Angie had to stop Miranda from upending a bucket of sand over the baby. The third time, she said, "I'm confiscating this," in a tone borrowed from every teacher she'd had since kindergarten, and set the bucket on top of the breakwater, out of Miranda's reach. Miranda cried. Jonathan, the five-year-old, climbed up after it and skinned his knee on a rock. At least he said he'd skinned it—Angie couldn't see any blood—and insisted he needed to go wash it off. By the time Angie realized she'd been conned, he was splashing around happily in water up to his waist. She yanked him out and dried him off, hoping maybe his mother wouldn't notice his wet suit. Meanwhile, Miranda had filled the bucket with pebbles from the base of the breakwater and was advancing on the baby again.

Angie took the bucket over to Mrs. Munson and asked if she'd mind keeping it on her lap. "Why, no, dear," Mrs. Munson said agreeably, setting her magazine aside again. "But it might be simpler if you just gave me the baby."

Though Angie could see the logic of this, she felt it would also mean losing part of her baby-sitting job to

Mrs. Munson. Besides, she needed to do something right away about Jonathan, who was digging a hole at the water's edge with Miranda's shovel and smearing gobs of black mud into Miranda's blond hair. Miranda didn't seem to mind the mud, but Angie had a feeling her mother might.

If her mother ever came back.

"Come on, let's go look at the ducks," Angie said.

She grabbed both kids by the hand and led them around the breakwater onto the grassy spit of land beyond. Meanwhile, she squinted across the dazzle of water to see if maybe the mother was lying on the raft and had fallen asleep there. On the other hand, maybe she'd decided to swim across the lake and climb Mt. Levêque while she had the chance. Angie decided she wouldn't necessarily blame her.

"I don't see any ducks," Jonathan complained in his stopped-up voice.

Angie released Miranda's hand long enough to point at random toward a reedy patch of water outside the ropes where there was a big submerged rock. "The ducks are in swimming," she said shamelessly. "See, there's the mommy duck and all the cute little baby ducks behind her. If you're real quiet, maybe they'll come back this way."

Miranda's mouth fell open. "Mommy!" she said. "Mommy's coming back."

Maybe the kid would grow up to be an astronomer

or something, Angie thought—she certainly had amazing eyesight. A faint, blurry shape that Angie had taken for a cruising turtle now resolved itself into a woman's head. No one ever swam ashore here, but with the kids yelling and waving and jumping up and down, Angie guessed the mother didn't have much choice. She did a careful breaststroke through all the reeds and climbed ashore, coated with muck from the bank. As she hugged the kids squelchily to her, saying "Goodness, you'd think I'd gone to China," Angie thought that at least she wasn't likely to notice Jonathan's wet suit or the mud in Miranda's hair.

"Oh, that was glorious!" she said to Angie as they all returned to the beach. "Is the baby still asleep?"

Angie nodded, though this was only an assumption. If the baby had awakened, she figured she would have heard it, if its lungs were anything like its sister's and brother's.

"So heavenly, getting off by myself for a few minutes," the mother went on as Angie surreptitiously retrieved Miranda's bucket from Mrs. Munson. "Now, how can I thank you?"

Angie was getting up the nerve to say that a couple of dollars would be fine when the woman said, "I know!" and stooped to rummage in one of the carrier bags surrounding her beach chair.

"I'm afraid it's a bit squashed," she said, handing Angie a plastic bag containing a lump of something that looked like more mud. "But that shouldn't affect the taste. Don't they make the most wonderful picnic lunches here?"

Angie identified the mud as a sorry-looking wedge of chocolate layer cake. Jonathan howled, "That's my dessert!" and made a grab for it. "I was saving it!"

"Now, Jonathan—"

"That's okay," Angie said, handing the bag back hastily. "I'm not too hungry right now, anyway."

"Well, have an apple, at least. I'm sure there's an apple here somewhere." The woman was rummaging again. "It might be a little bruised, but—"

"Thanks," Angie said bleakly. "But I think I'll just go for a swim."

Chapter

✳ ✳ ✳

L istening to Rita Crawford do her archery practice was a lot like listening to Hugh Curtis hit a tennis ball, Angie decided—it was a long time between the thumps that meant Rita had actually hit the target. Angie wondered where all the other arrows were landing, but figured she was safe enough here outside the gate. Unless, of course, Rita turned around for some reason and started shooting in the opposite direction.

Because of all the bushes and tall grass inside the archery enclosure, Angie couldn't actually see Rita from where she sat, hunkered down against the fence, with beetles investigating her ankles and her jeans getting soaked with dew. When anyone came along the road or the cabin path above it, she pretended to be reading a book she'd brought along. So far the only person who'd noticed her was Pierre, the elderly French-Canadian man-of-all-work, trundling a wheelbarrow load of stove ashes from the far cabins to spread on Nora's flower beds. He'd looked a little surprised to see Angie there—certainly the sunny porch of Cedar Waxwing would have been a more comfortable place to read—but had only smiled, said, "Morning, missy," and gone on his way.

Angie yawned and brushed a caterpillar off her knee. It was the hour after breakfast, when most people were getting organized for the day. It was also the hour Rita devoted to morning archery practice, which was why Angie was stuck here waiting for her to finish. She needed to speak to Rita alone, before she got involved in another of her mysterious Western-style activities, like roping tree stumps with her lariat or taking a beeline hike through the woods, marching through poison ivy and mudholes and brier patches without allowing herself to detour or even flinch.

Angie's own plan for the day was a simple one, at least compared to yesterday's. All the placard in her head said was: BORROW MONEY FROM RITA.

This brilliant solution to her problem had burst upon her earlier that morning, when she was lying in bed in Cedar Waxwing trying to remember why she didn't feel happier about waking up at Potter's on another beautiful summer day, with eight whole days of vacation still to go. Once she did remember, eight days didn't seem like very much at all. For a panicky moment Angie had considered creeping into the living room to see if there might just happen to be $14.84 in her mother's handbag. If there was and she took it, her mother might not even notice its absence, since she was even vaguer about money than Angie was. When Angie got her September allowance, she could slip the money back, and her mother might not notice that, either.

But no, Angie had told herself sternly, that would only be compounding her crime. If she was going to borrow money, the other person had to *know* about it. Then she'd sat up in bed wide-eyed, wondering why this idea hadn't occurred to her before. There was nothing wrong with borrowing from someone who could spare the money and who wouldn't necessarily want to know what she needed it for. The person would have to be a kid, of course—an adult would insist on knowing. Who did she know that didn't have any curiosity?

Angie had thought first of her cousin Gus, whose curiosity was pretty much limited to fish—where they hung out, what kind of mood they were in, and what kind of fly or bug they might feel like eating. But Gus had just bought a new leader for his line, so he probably wouldn't have any money.

A few minutes' further thought showed Angie the perfect person, someone she didn't know very well and who wouldn't be likely to blab to Angie's family in the months to come, since she lived two thousand miles away in Colorado: Rita Crawford.

With relief, Angie had mentally ripped up and thrown away yesterday's plan, which just hadn't worked out at all.

She'd been right in thinking there were plenty of odd jobs around. In fact, once she'd set off on their trail, new possibilities seemed to spring up at every turn, like grouse from cover. The problem was that no one seemed to think of money in connection with any of them.

On her way back from Great Harriman, for instance, Angie had stopped off at the stables and spent a hot, sticky hour helping Karen clean tack. Karen was the college girl who was in charge of the horses and who took people on trail rides. She'd handed Angie a rag and a can of saddle soap and spent most of the hour talking about her boyfriend back home in Maryland. She seemed to assume Angie was just another horse-crazy kid who liked hanging around the stables. Never mind that until now Angie had rarely shown up for a ride in time to saddle her horse, let alone stuck around afterward to take off the bridle and rinse the yucky bit under the tap.

"Well, been good talkin' to you," Karen had said after they'd finished the last pair of reins. When Angie made no move to leave but stood looking at her expectantly, the way she'd practiced, Karen added with a wink, "Maybe I can sneak you an extra fifteen minutes on Belly Dancer sometime. Not supposed to give out free rides, but what the hey, I don't always need to look at my watch, right?"

Belly Dancer was the horse Angie usually rode, a bay mare presently regarding them solemnly over the half door of its stall. While Angie turned and stroked its nose dutifully—she liked riding, especially when Karen let them gallop, but horses themselves didn't interest her much—she did a quick computation. At the rate Karen charged per hour, the price of a fifteen-minute ride would go a good way toward making up the missing $14.84. Could she just ask Karen to give her the money instead? Regretfully, Angie decided she couldn't.

At least Karen's offer had been a kind of thanks, which was more than Angie got later from old Mr. Jeffries' nurse—or from Mr. Jeffries himself, for that matter. Seeing the nurse knitting grimly on the shady front porch of Merganser, the small cabin Mr. Jeffries occupied with his schnauzer, Fritz, Angie had had what she thought was an inspired idea: What if she offered to read to the old man for a while so the nurse could take a break?

Surely the nurse would be grateful, considering how much she seemed to hate her job. Angie knew she had plenty of money, because she was always complaining about the lack of decent shops in this godforsaken part of the world. She also knew that Mr. Jeffries liked being read to, since this was one of the ways the nurse got him to do what she wanted. "No Dickens tonight if we don't behave ourselves," she'd been heard to growl when he refused to take his medicine or wanted to go to dinner in his bathrobe or have Fritz sleep on his bed.

The nurse had narrowed her eyes suspiciously at Angie but said, "Okay, if you got nothing better to do," and clomped off the porch with her knitting bag slung over her shoulder like an ammunition pouch.

Angie found Mr. Jeffries sitting in the tiny living room with Fritz at his feet. At first, neither of them seemed to know who she was. Only when Angie picked up the book lying open on the windowsill did Fritz stop snarling and snapping at her ankles. Mr. Jeffries blinked at her and said, "Ah, yes, pretty little Angie, how delightful." He settled back to listen, adjusting his glasses on his nose and folding his liver-spotted hands over his paunch.

The book was about an old guy named Mr. Pickwick who sounded a little like Mr. Jeffries himself but who seemed to be a lot more with it, in spite of all the confusing things that were happening in the story. Of course, Angie had started in the middle. Also the print was really small, with lots of hard words in it. After a while, she started leaving out some of the longer ones. Fritz had begun snoring so loudly that she doubted Mr. Jeffries could hear very well, anyway. A few minutes later, she saw that Mr. Jeffries, too, was asleep.

Angie had gone on reading, though, since that was

what she'd told the nurse she was going to do. Well, sort of reading. Soon she was skipping whole lines, even whole paragraphs, and fighting yawns as she turned the pages. All the sleepiness was contagious. Besides, it was stuffy in the little room, with the sunlight beginning to slant down over the wooded ridge behind the cabin. When the nurse came back, mounting the porch steps with a tread that made the whole structure quiver, Angie rose with alacrity and returned the book to the windowsill.

Unfortunately, she'd forgotten to mark the place. "Well, that's a fine how'd-you-do," the nurse had grumbled. "*He* won't remember where you left off, and I'm certainly not going to start the thing all over from the beginning." She cracked the book open in the middle and slammed it face down with a bang that made Angie wince. "There, that'll do," she said, and glared at Angie. "Well, what're you hanging around for?"

Angie had opened her mouth, closed it again, and beat a hasty retreat.

Chapter

✳ ✳ ✳

Not only had she received no pay and no thanks, Angie thought now as she waited for Rita to finish her archery practice, she seemed to have picked up some fleas from Fritz. Surely plain old beetles wouldn't be making her ankles itch like this.

But the worst thing about yesterday had been the way word had spread of Angie's good deeds, as people insisted on thinking of them. The last of these had been putting the croquet set away at the end of the afternoon, in full view of everyone on the lodge veranda. In this case, Angie hadn't expected to be paid—it was just that she'd tripped over a wicket at dusk the night before and almost wrecked her ankle. At dinner, Steve had asked her if she was running for saint. Their parents had rebuked him, saying there was nothing wrong with being a thoughtful, caring person.

But Angie had seen them exchange a worried glance.

Well, never mind. In another few minutes, all her problems would be solved, and she could go back to being her ordinary, carefree self instead of a person weighed down with a guilty secret. In fact—Angie stopped scratching her ankles and cocked her head—it had been a while now since she'd heard the twang of Rita's bow, let alone the thump of an arrow hitting the target. Cautiously she got to her feet and pushed through the gate.

"Hi, Rita," she said brightly to Rita's back. "It's me, Angie." Rita was at the rear of the enclosure, poking around with her bow in a tangle of goldenrod and tall pink fireweed. "You all done for now?"

"Sort of," Rita said over her shoulder. "I only have one arrow left, and I guess I better not shoot it in case I lose that one too."

"You lost all those arrows?" Angie was astonished. When she'd seen Rita marching along the road an hour ago, the quiver over her shoulder had been bristling with blue- and red-feathered arrows.

"Yeah. I guess a bunch of them went over the fence. I'm getting real strong because of practicing so much, but my aim . . ." Rita shook her head, giving a twitch to the long ginger-blond braid that hung down between her shoulder blades. "I hope I didn't shoot too many in the lake. Some of the arrows are mine, but the others, the ones with the red feathers, belong to Potter's."

Angie didn't offer to help Rita look for the arrows—she'd learned her lesson about volunteer work. Instead she said craftily, "Well, I guess you can always buy a new set. I mean, it's not like you ever spend any of your allowance."

"Right." Rita turned and frowned at Angie. She was wearing bright green shorts and a pink T-shirt that was almost the same shade as the fireweed—Angie's least-favorite color combination. "How do you know?"

Angie had to think. "Well, your grandmother always pays if we go bowling in Gilead." Gilead was the nearest town of any size, over the border in New Hampshire. On rainy afternoons, Ray sometimes piled a bunch of kids in the truck and took them to the bowling alley there. "And she lets you charge ice cream and stuff at Marie's. And on bingo nights, you never play more than five cards." At a nickel a card, Angie figured bingo couldn't be making too many inroads on Rita's allowance.

Rita nodded. "Yeah, well, I never have any luck at bingo. I take after Gran that way, I guess." Mrs. Rowan's bad luck at bingo was a Potter's legend—she'd gone about fifteen years without a single winning card.

"So anyway," Angie said briskly, "I figured you'd be a good person to ask for a loan."

Rita had been in the act of unstringing her bow. Now she lowered it to her side and stared at Angie.

"A loan? You mean a loan of *money*?" She spoke as if Angie had asked her to cut off her right arm.

"Well, yeah," Angie said, trying not to show her dismay at this reaction. "Not a whole lot of money," she explained hastily, "and I'd pay you back the first week in September. I could even FedEx it to you, if you want." When Rita still stared at her, she said, "I guess I could pay extra, too. You know, add on what's-it-called—"

"Interest," Rita supplied, and added, "I don't think you're allowed to send money through the mail—not unless it's a check. But anyway, I don't. Lend money, I mean." Her expression had gone flat, reminding Angie of someone, she couldn't think who.

Angie looked at her helplessly. "But if you have money you're not using, and someone else really *needs* it—" She broke off, reminding herself that the last thing she wanted was to have Rita start asking why she needed money.

But Rita didn't. She just shrugged and said, "It's the way I was raised. You start lending people money, pretty soon you have a big hassle trying to keep track of where it all is. It's just easier if you hang on to it yourself."

Now Angie knew who Rita reminded her of, with her pale hazel eyes and her stubborn, rather slablike jaw—old Ephraim Potter, Mr. Moneybags himself, whose portrait hung in the lodge. He had to be some kind of relation of Rita's, she realized, since Mrs. Rowan was his niece.

"I might *buy* something," Rita observed, dropping her one remaining arrow into the empty quiver. "I mean, if you had anything to sell that I wanted." She paused. "It would have to be something new, though. I wouldn't buy anything *used*."

Was that another of Rita's family rules? But never mind—what did Angie have that was new that Rita might want? She thought of her shiny new baton (except her mother had made her leave it at home, saying they all needed a vacation from Angie in the role of whirling dervish), of her fire-engine-red T-shirt from the PTA fair (except that would look really terrible with Rita's hair and freckles). Finally, with a sense of inevitability, she thought of the horror video in its hiding place under the floorboards of Cedar Waxwing.

"Wait here," she told Rita. "I've got something you're going to love."

Chapter

✳ ✳ ✳

Angie was pretty sure the cabin would be empty at this hour. Steve was going sailing on Great Harriman, and her parents were driving down to Island Pond to have lunch with friends who had a vacation house there. Still, she thought it wise to make a commando circuit of the hillside, tunneling down through a grove of hemlocks so she could sneak into Cedar Waxwing by the narrow back door no one ever used.

Once in her room, she couldn't remember which floorboard was the loose one. She was sure the video was still there, though—hadn't she almost heard it beating in the middle of the night, like the telltale heart in that spooky story they'd read in school? She made herself close her eyes and open them again. Right, the second board in from the corner, beyond the window. She pried it up, dusted off the vinyl cover of the video with the tail of her shirt, and dashed back down the hill.

"Here," she said breathlessly, bursting through the gate.

Once again Rita had her back turned. She was standing beside the wheel of hay that served as a target, calling to someone Angie couldn't see in the tangle of brush beyond the back fence.

"Over to the right more, where that tree is. There might be one in the tree trunk, too, the way the squirrels were acting so scared." As Angie thrust the video into her hands, Rita frowned and said, "Oh, wow, I hope I didn't *hit* a squirrel." She stared down at the video. "What's this? It looks creepy."

"Right," Angie said enthusiastically. "It might be one of the creepiest movies ever made. It might even make you throw up."

"But what's it called?" Rita pointed to the title, a series of jagged letters imposed on a picture of some swollen, slimy-looking monsters with blood dripping from their mouths.

"I don't know," Angie said with a shrug. "It's in French, I guess. I got it up in Quebec. But look." She turned the case over to show Rita the picture on the back, in which a family of humans lay pale and limp as flour sacks on the edge of a black pond. "Doesn't it look *gross*?"

"Is all the talking going to be in French too?"

"I guess. But so what? If it's scary enough, you won't even hear the talking—you'll be screaming too loud."

Rita shook her head doubtfully. "I don't know any French," she said. "And if you haven't even watched it yet, how do you know it's any good?"

"Rita, you said it had to be something *new*," Angie said in exasperation. "Besides, how could I watch it here, where there isn't even a VCR? There's only that old TV in the lodge that you can't even tune in if it's raining. Unless your grandmother has a VCR," she added hopefully, thinking maybe she might get to see the video after all.

Rita shook her head again. She stood considering, chewing on the end of her braid. Finally she said, "How much?"

"Fourteen dollars and eighty-four cents," Angie said promptly. She saw Rita looking at the price sticker on the corner of the video and explained hastily, "That's in francs, but fourteen dollars and eighty-four cents is what it comes to in American money."

"Well, it isn't brand-new," Rita said, running her thumb critically down the spine. "I mean, you've had it a while, right? So it's not brand-new from the store. And also I'm not all that big on horror movies. I like Westerns better, the old kind with cowboys and Indians—I mean Native Americans—in them. You know?"

Angie nodded dutifully. The suspense was killing her.

"And also I'd have to hide it from Gran. She thinks stuff like this is real tacky." Angie nodded again. That was fine with her. Mrs. Rowan was a friend of her parents, and the last thing she needed was Mrs. Rowan asking Rita where she'd gotten the video. "So I'll give you half."

Angie sagged. "Half?"

"Whatever half of fourteen eighty-four is."

"Seven dollars and forty-two cents," Angie said automatically. "But Rita—"

"That's my offer," Rita said, picking up her bow. "Take it or leave it."

Angie looked at the set of Rita's jaw and knew it was no use arguing. "Okay," she said with a sigh. At least she was $7.42 ahead of where she'd been before. "But listen, that's still not all the money I need. I still need . . . well, seven forty-two."

As she tucked the video under her arm, Rita gave Angie a thoughtful look. If she made the connection, though, she didn't say so. Instead she said, "You have anything else to sell?"

Angie thought. "A tube of pimple cream?" she offered. But Rita, who was a year or two younger, looked blank. "Okay," Angie said reluctantly, "how about a neat red T-shirt that's never been worn? I got it at a fair we had at school. It says 'All Poor Spellers Go to Heven' on the back. 'Heaven' is spelled wrong," she explained. "It's a joke, sort of." She didn't think it necessary to add that it was a joke that had to be explained to her by Courtney, who was a better speller.

Rita didn't smile. "I hardly ever wear red," she said dismissively. "Bright colors make me sweat. But anyway, that would only be worth three dollars. Maybe three fifty."

Before Angie could protest that the T-shirt had cost her a whole $9.50 plus tax, also that the shade of pink Rita had on was as bright as any color she'd ever seen away from MTV, Rita added, "Speaking of school reminds me of something, though."

"What?" Angie asked, without much hope.

Rita looked down, scuffing at a weed with the dusty toe of her hiking boot. "Well, see, there's this project we have to do over the summer. It's supposed to be something creative. My school makes us do one every year."

"So?" Creative projects were the kind Angie liked. They were usually a lot easier than regular ones.

"So I don't know what to do, and I need to start working on it. Last year I whittled a family of chipmunks, and it turned out real good. You've seen my whittling, right?"

Angie nodded. Rita was always leaving small, chewed-looking lumps of wood out on the railing of the lodge veranda. It had become a kind of game with the other kids to guess what they were supposed to represent.

"I'd whittle something else this year—rabbits maybe, or turtles—except you're not allowed to do the same kind of thing twice. So then I thought of doing a research project with crayfish, only they died." Rita sighed heavily. "And I'm no good at painting pictures or modeling stuff out of clay or making up songs. I guess I could yodel something, but Gran won't let me yodel anymore unless I go way off in the woods, so it's hard to practice."

Angie nodded sympathetically—her mother was the same way about baton practice—and swallowed a yawn. She couldn't imagine where all this was leading, and she was beginning to feel a bit bored.

"Anyway, I decided the easiest thing would be to write a story, only I can't think of anything to write about." Rita raised her head and gave Angie an earnest look through her sandy lashes. "Maybe you could help me think of something." As Angie gaped at her, she explained, "Like, you're artistic, you know? I mean, you're into stuff like dancing and acting in plays. What I need is someone with *imagination*, see, like I don't have. I already asked Wanda," she added before Angie could say anything, "but she's worried it would be cheating."

Angie found her voice. "You mean you want me to write a story for you?"

"No, no." Rita frowned. "I'd do the writing part—putting down the words and everything. It really *would* be cheating if I got someone else to write it. I just need you to make up the ideas."

"Well, good," Angie said before she thought, "because I'm not too great on commas and periods and stuff like that." She stared at Rita as it dawned on her that she was actually being offered a job. "And you'd pay me to help you with the idea part?"

Rita nodded. "Seven dollars and forty-five cents."

"Seven forty-two," Angie corrected her, and blew out her breath in a perplexed sigh. She'd told herself she was through trying to earn the money back, but this . . . "Well, sure. I mean, why not?"

Rita looked pleased—as pleased as she ever did, anyway. She shouldered her bow and quiver and stuck out her right hand. "Deal?" she said.

"Deal," Angie agreed dazedly, shaking Rita's hand. She thought for a moment. "But what if you don't like my ideas?"

"I guess we'd just keep going," Rita said with a shrug, "until you thought up one I liked."

Angie decided she'd think about this potential problem later. She said, "When do you want to start?"

Rita considered. "Well, I don't want Gran to know what we're doing," she said. "I mean, it's not cheating— at least I don't think it is—but Gran might think I should be making up the story all by myself. So maybe we should meet tomorrow morning before breakfast, when she'll be out bird-watching."

Before breakfast wasn't Angie's best time for doing anything, let alone anything creative, but she felt she'd better not say so. They made a date for six fifteen the next morning, at Mrs. Rowan's cabin. (Six fifteen!) Then Rita gave another hitch to her bow and quiver, thrust the video out of sight under her T-shirt—just as Angie herself had done, she couldn't help thinking a little wistfully—and strode away.

Chapter

✳ ✳ ✳

Left alone in the sunny clearing, Angie felt suddenly lightheaded with relief. She'd actually done it—she'd solved her money problem! In another day or so, she'd be able to return the whole $14.84 to the cashbox and go on with her vacation as if nothing had happened. And really, when you came right down to it, nothing had. The bills and coins might not be the exact same ones she'd started out with, but so what? The nice thing about money, Angie thought, was that it told no tales.

To celebrate, she threw herself into a series of pirouettes around the target, noticing as she did so that its vinyl bull's-eye was only sparsely punctured with arrow holes. Apparently no one except Rita was into archery this year. Getting dizzy, Angie switched routines and went into a high-stepping strut, tossing an imaginary baton high in the air and catching it again, whirling it behind her back, up over her shoulder, under one leg, then under the other—

"I heard," said a voice behind her.

Angie spun around. Hugh Curtis was standing in the gateway, clutching a fistful of arrows. His oversized T-shirt hung off one shoulder, his baggy shorts were puckered with burrs and thistles, and there was a muddy scrape on one knobby knee. There was nothing unusual about any of that. What *was* unusual was the look of determination on Hugh's face.

"What are you doing here?" Angie demanded faintly. She had a strong feeling that Hugh was not going to be good news.

"Rita asked me to help find her arrows. I guess she forgot." Hugh shrugged, and Angie nodded in spite of herself. People were always forgetting about Hugh. "But anyway, I heard what you guys were saying, and about how it's supposed to be a secret from Mrs. Rowan." He paused. "I don't know what it *is*, exactly, but I know it's a secret."

"Right." Angie gave him her most winning smile. "And I bet you're good at keeping secrets, aren't you, Hugh?"

Hugh shook his head. "I'll tell," he said. "I'll tell everyone you and Rita are doing something sneaky."

"It's nothing *sneaky*, Hugh," Angie began. "Not like you mean. It's—"

But Hugh wasn't finished. "Unless you give me canoe lessons," he said. When Angie just stared at him, her head beginning to buzz as though a swarm of bees had gotten loose inside it, he explained clearly, "I want to learn how to row a canoe. You're the best kid here at canoeing—well, except Steve, but I know he'd never help me—so you're the one I want to teach me. And if you won't, I'll tell."

And that, it seemed, was all Hugh had to say. Nothing Angie could come up with—that managing a canoe was tricky, that you needed to be a good swimmer first, that you needed to be *coordinated*, for Pete's sake—would shake him.

Finally she said with a groan, "Okay, but only three lessons. If you can't get the hang of it by then, that's it." She drew a deep breath, thinking furiously. "And the lessons have got to be a secret too." Angie didn't know how she was going to manage this, only that no one would believe she was giving Hugh Curtis canoe lessons of her own free will.

"Well, sure," Hugh said, wide-eyed, letting several arrows fall to the ground. He was beginning to look more like his usual self, his mouth hanging slightly open, his knees and elbows flexing as if an invisible puppeteer were twitching his strings. "My aunt and uncle would never let me go *canoeing*. They don't even like me going out in a rowboat by myself."

Mr. and Mrs. Curtis were a stolid, slow-moving

couple who rarely ventured off the path between their cabin and the lodge and who certainly never messed around with water sports. Angie didn't know where Hugh's parents were. She had a vague idea the Curtises might have adopted him for some bizarre reason.

Angie sighed. Here she'd found someone who wanted to take lessons from her, and not only wouldn't she be paid, she'd probably be in big trouble if anyone ever found out about them.

"When can we start?" Hugh said, bouncing on the balls of his feet. "Hey, what about right now?" Angie glared at him. "Or after lunch?"

Angie informed him tersely that she was taking the rest of the day off. Hugh didn't ask what she was taking it off from, and Angie didn't explain. They settled on the next morning after breakfast, when Hugh said his aunt and uncle would be off doing errands. Hugh insisted they shake hands and say "Deal," the way she and Rita had. Then he collected the arrows he'd dropped and marched importantly up the road to deliver them to Rita at Mrs. Rowan's cabin near the head of the lake.

Angie wiped her hand on her jeans and stood glowering after Hugh's retreating figure. With any luck, she thought, he'd trip over his own feet and stab himself with an arrow or two. Not badly enough to draw blood, she amended hastily. Just enough to keep him out of a canoe for the next few days.

* * *

As Angie's Uncle Maury arrived at the dinner table that evening, he produced a medium-sized book from the pocket of his sport coat. "Is this yours, Angie?" he inquired, handing it across the table. "I found it in the grass by the side of the road, near the archery range. Didn't seem like anything you'd be carrying around with you, but it has your initials in front."

Angie winced as Steve leaned over and read the title. "Your social-studies book?" he said incredulously. Angie hadn't even noticed which book it was—she'd just grabbed it from the pile of stuff on the floor of her closet. Certainly she hadn't *read* it. "Boy, you're getting really weird, you know?"

Just wait till he saw her hanging around with the likes of Rita Crawford and Hugh Curtis, Angie thought gloomily.

"Really, Angie," her mother said. "We lugged those books up here so you could do some studying before school starts, the way Mr. Walker suggested, not so you could leave them lying around getting rained on."

"It isn't raining," Angie objected lamely.

"It's supposed to rain tonight, though," Gus said. "Not hard." He looked pleased. No one had to ask why. They all knew he was thinking about good fishing weather.

"Well, there you are," Mrs. Hyatt said. "And with the price of books these days, we can't afford to replace them before school even starts."

Angie's father laughed, leaning back in his chair. "I'm glad you know the price of books, dear, because you certainly don't seem overly concerned with the price of shoes. The bill I got today for a pair of sandals—" He shook his head. "A few little straps of leather, but they might as well be platinum."

"Now, Jack," said his wife, stretching out a long leg to admire her elegantly shod foot, "they've already come in very handy. Besides, they'll last forever. Right, Marge?"

Her sister nodded, but murmured, "Except who wants to wear anything forever?"

"And besides that, I'm on vacation, and I refuse to think about money when I'm on vacation. Yes, I know I brought the subject up, but consider it scratched. Time enough to worry about bills when we get home. Oh, sorry, Melissa, I didn't mean to trip you," she said to the waitress, who'd appeared to take their order.

Mr. Hyatt said with an indulgent smile, "The only problem with that, dear, is you're *always* on vacation, one way or another. But never mind, I love you anyway."

Angie didn't think this was quite fair. Her mother had a part-time job at a travel agency back home, though it was true she went out to lunch a lot.

But Mrs. Hyatt only returned the smile and gave her attention to the typed menu, tucking her blond hair behind her ears. It was sleeker than Angie's hair and several shades darker, but Angie supposed hers would look like that when she grew up. People were always saying she was the image of her mother, just as they said Steve was the image of his father. In their case, it wasn't so much their appearance—Steve was blond too, while their father had curly brown hair, beginning to recede on top—as their expressions, the way they always looked so alert and combative and ready to get to the bottom of things.

Matched pairs, Angie thought. She found herself resenting the idea for the first time, though she wasn't sure why. She loved her mother, after all. If she just sort of floated pleasantly through life, as Steve sometimes said, what was wrong with that?

"I'll have the roast lamb," Mrs. Hyatt told Melissa. "With the garlic sauce, I think, rather than the mint gravy."

"So will I," Aunt Marge said, and sneezed. "Darn, I think I'm getting the cold that's going around."

Steve said, "Maybe you could get them to put some extra garlic in the sauce."

His aunt looked at him resignedly. "Why?"

"Because garlic's supposed to be good for colds."

"I thought it was for warding off demons," Uncle Maury said, giving Angie a wink. "You string a big smelly head of garlic around your neck, and *presto*, all your troubles just melt away."

Everyone laughed. Angie said "Yuck" a little warily,

hoping he didn't mean her in particular. Uncle Maury was a lawyer, good at spotting people in trouble. At the same time, she couldn't help thinking that a head of garlic might be worth a try. At the very least, it might keep Hugh Curtis at a distance when she had to get into a canoe with him.

Chapter

✻ ✻ ✻

H ey, this is neat," Angie said, pausing in the doorway of Mrs. Rowan's cabin. She'd never been inside before, only sat on the porch sometimes when Mrs. Rowan invited her parents over for drinks. "Like a regular *home*."

There was a beige carpet, and a real sofa with flowered cushions, and end tables with matching lamps. The usual Potter's wood stove occupied a corner of the living room, but there was also a heating duct along one wall.

Rita said, "I guess Gran spends practically half the year here. Not when it's really snowy, though. She says no one can even get in to Potter's then unless they have a snowmobile." She thought for a moment. "Course, you could always trek in on snowshoes. Only that's harder than it looks, especially if you're packing a lot of gear."

Angie nodded absently. She'd tried snowshoeing once, and had gotten herself into a lock—one heel piece clamped over the other—from which it had taken two people, Steve and her father, to extricate her.

"Where does she live the rest of the time?" she asked, examining a group of framed photographs on the wall above the couch. One was of a distinguished-looking man in a tuxedo sitting at a gleaming piano, throwing an equally gleaming smile over his shoulder. It was signed *"To Miriam, with love,"* though Angie couldn't make out the signature.

"I don't know," Rita said. "In Ohio, I think, or maybe it's Iowa. I get all these eastern states mixed up." She scooped a little pile of bills and coins off a table and handed them to Angie. "This is for the video. Sorry I had to use so many pennies."

Angie stared at Rita as she stuffed the money into the pocket of her jeans. "You don't *know?*" She herself didn't see a whole lot of her grandparents, but their whereabouts were firmly fixed in her mind—her father's parents in a sunny retirement community outside Tucson, Arizona, her mother's parents in a tall brick house in Baltimore.

"Well, see, I never even met Gran till I came here. She and my mom don't get along," Rita explained, "so they stopped being in touch way back when. You could have knocked my mom over with a feather when Gran wrote and invited me to Potter's. That's what Mom said, except I can't see a feather really knocking someone over, can you? Unless maybe it came from an eagle."

Angie was intrigued. "Wow, a real family what-d'you-call-it, a *feud*," she exclaimed. She couldn't imagine being out of touch with her own mother, even when she was grown up. For all her casual ways, her mother would be sure to keep tabs on her, reminding Angie to clean her house and get off the phone and eat something besides junk food. "What happened? I mean, why don't they get along?"

Rita shook her head. "It has something to do with my grandfather, that's all I know." She produced a new-looking spiral pad and a sharpened pencil and sat down at the end of the dining table next to the kitchen door. "Okay," she said, "I'm ready. We'll number all your ideas. Then we'll narrow them down and choose the best one."

But Angie was not to be diverted. No one at Potter's had ever met Mrs. Rowan's husband, nor did Mrs. Rowan ever mention him. Angie had heard her parents and her aunt and uncle speculating about what had happened to the mysterious Mr. Rowan. Opinion was divided between death, divorce, and disappearance. Since Mrs. Rowan was an easygoing kind of person with no visible peculiarities except her love of bird-watching, they'd pretty much opted for an early death, perhaps a gruesome one—something so painful that Mrs. Rowan couldn't bring herself to speak of it.

"Does she have any pictures of him?" Angie asked, looking again at the photographs on the wall. One lady seemed vaguely familiar, a pretty older woman wearing a ball gown and a diamond necklace, with a matching tiara set on top of her shapely, gray-blond head.

"Of who?"

"Your grandfather."

"Not that I've seen. We have some at home, though—real old ones. He used to be an explorer, I think. Or maybe some kind of scientist who had to travel a lot. Or he might have been something in the Navy. There's a lot of rocks and water in the pictures," she explained.

An explorer! Angie thought, automatically dismissing the less glamorous possibilities. Just wait till she told her parents! Here was an explanation that could account for two out of their three conjectures—death and disappearance. Maybe Mr. Rowan (Commander Rowan? That sounded better.) had vanished on an expedition to the Arctic or the Antarctic or wherever. Right, and his body had never been recovered, in spite of searches with dogsleds and kayaks and maybe even helicopters, depending on how long ago it all was. . . .

Except that wouldn't necessarily explain the rift in the family, Angie thought. Also, she might be getting ahead of herself. "Used to be?" she said. "You mean he's dead?"

Rita considered, chewing on the tail of her braid. "I don't think so. I'm pretty sure Mom gets cards from him sometimes, on her birthday and at Christmas." She flipped the braid back over her shoulder and picked up her pencil. "So what's your first idea?"

Angie stared at her. "Aren't you even *curious*?" she demanded. "About your grandparents and your mother and the feud and everything?"

When Rita just looked at her blankly, Angie remembered that Rita's lack of curiosity was the whole reason she'd gotten mixed up with her in the first place. She sighed in frustration. "Okay, but first do you have any juice?"

Rita frowned. "Listen, Angie, I really need to get going on my project." She consulted the large watch strapped to her wrist. It was a stopwatch, Angie knew. She hoped Rita hadn't set the timer. "It's starting to rain again, and if it rains hard enough so the birds all go under the leaves or back to their nests, Gran won't stay out the way she usually does."

True to Gus's forecast, a gentle drizzle had begun during the night and looked as if it might continue on and off all day.

"I can't think on an empty stomach," Angie protested, stalling for time, though it was true that her insides felt hollow. She'd eaten a couple of stale Ritz crackers she'd found in a jacket pocket, but she hadn't dared forage in the living room for the fruit and cookies they sometimes saved from picnic lunches, in case Steve woke up and asked where she was going.

"You mean you're only just now starting to think up stuff?" Rita frowned again, reminding Angie that this was, after all, a paying job.

"Oh, no, I've already had a couple of good ideas," she said hastily. "Like you could write a story about a kid who lives out West and comes East for the first time and has to, you know, adjust to everything being so different. . . . Look, if there's some juice in the fridge, I can just help myself. Or let's see," Angie went on, edging past Rita into the small, tidy kitchen and swinging open the refrigerator door, "you could write about a kid who's trying to learn archery, only her aim isn't too good, and she keeps losing all her arrows. . . ."

There was a jar of apple juice in the fridge, and an open package of English muffins that Angie eyed hungrily. But no, this wasn't the moment to start toasting things. She found a glass in a cupboard, filled it with juice, and returned to the living room.

Rita had a scowl on her face, and Angie noticed she hadn't written anything down on her pad. She said, "Hey, I'm not gonna write anything about *myself*."

"Why not?" Angie looked at her in surprise. "My English teacher's always saying you should write about stuff you really know. And who do you know better than your own self?"

She took a swallow of her juice and sat down on the

couch. It was really comfortable, especially compared to the battered wicker settee in Cedar Waxwing with its three limp plaid cushions.

"That's what I always do when I have to write a composition," Angie explained as Rita continued to scowl. "Of course, I add stuff out of my imagination," she said quickly, in case Rita might feel she wouldn't be getting her money's worth. "Like with the archery story, there could be a tournament you were practicing for, with a trophy and everything. And you'd really need to win it, see, because if you *didn't*—"

She paused impressively, trying to think what dire thing might happen if Rita still couldn't hit the target. The tournament part was easy, because Potter's had sometimes held them in past years, with everyone divided up according to age. There'd never been a trophy, though, just homemade prize ribbons that Nora lettered with gold paint and glued pinecones to for rosettes. Steve had several blue ones gathering dust over his mirror at home.

But Rita wanted no part of this scenario. "I'm a real private person," she informed Angie. "I'd never even keep a diary, in case the twins might find it and read it. Course, I wouldn't put anything *personal* in it, only stuff about the weather and what I had to eat, but still—" She sighed. "I guess being private is another way I'm like Gran."

Another way? Angie tried to think what the first one

was. Oh, yes, being unlucky at bingo. A tiny bell sounded in the back of her mind. What was it someone had said about Mrs. Rowan, one night before bingo?

But she couldn't remember, and anyway, she was distracted by Rita's mention of twins. Twins fascinated Angie, who thought she would have enjoyed having a mirror-image self, someone to giggle with and tell secrets to.

"I thought you just had older brothers," she said. "Are they the kind that look exactly alike, so even their own family can't tell them apart?"

"Who?"

"The twins." Angie managed not to roll her eyes, the way Steve was always doing to her. If he thought Angie was hard to talk to, he should try having a conversation with Rita.

"Oh, they're just my cousins," Rita said. "They only live a couple of blocks from us, though, so they're always hanging around." Angie blinked. Somehow she'd gotten the idea that Rita lived on a ranch out in the middle of nowhere. "But yeah, they're identical twins, only you can tell them apart easy because one has braces and the other doesn't." Before Angie could point out that this wasn't a difference that would last forever, Rita turned back to her spiral pad and said, "Okay, what other ideas did you have?"

Angie rummaged rapidly through the untidy contents of her mind.

"Well, you could write a description," she suggested. "This doesn't have to be a story with people in it, does it?" Rita shook her head uncertainly. "So you could describe—oh, Heron Lake, with the water lilies and the beaver dam and the herons and everything. By moonlight, maybe, and put in lots of what-d'you-call-'em, adjectives. Except I guess the herons might not be out then." She paused. "Or I know, how about Dark Pool? That'd be a neat place to describe, and you were there just the day before yesterday." Angie sighed, still regretting her missed excursion.

Rita looked doubtful, but at least she wrote these ideas down. Meanwhile Angie finished her juice, set the glass down on the coffee table, and swung around so she could lie back and drape her legs over the arm of the couch—her best position for thinking. From this vantage point, she also had a fresh view of the framed photos above her head.

"Hey!" she said, squinting up at the woman in the ball gown. "That's that movie star, the one that married a prince! And then she died in a car crash—that was so sad. Grace Kelly, right?" Now she could see that the picture was inscribed in one corner with the words "*All the best to Mim from G.*"

Rita followed her glance. "Right," she said, without interest. "Gran went to school with her or something."

"Really? They were *friends*? Wow! I mean, Grace Kelly was famous!"

"Well, she wasn't famous then," Rita pointed out. "And I guess everyone has to go to school."

But Angie sat up, galvanized by a genuine idea. "Listen, Rita, I know what you should write about. 'The Most Fascinating Character I Ever Met.' Teachers love that kind of stuff. I don't mean Grace Kelly," she said hastily, as Rita opened her mouth to protest that she'd never met Grace Kelly. "I mean your grandmother."

Chapter

❋ ❋ ❋

Gran?" Rita frowned. "But she's not famous or rich or anything. I mean, I think she's real nice, but—"

"The person doesn't have to be famous," Angie interrupted. "Just fascinating. And look at all the stuff your grandmother's done—being married to an explorer and meeting celebrities and going on trips. . . . I bet she's been lots of different places, right?" Angie was on her feet now, prowling around the room in search of further clues. Sure enough, there was an African-looking mask on the wall behind the stove, and a beaded cushion on a rocking chair that looked as if it might have come from someplace like India.

"Mostly just to look at birds," Rita said, but she was writing on the pad again.

"Well, sure, and you could tell about her bird-watching, too—how she's won prizes for seeing more birds than anyone else, or different birds, or whatever. Or if she didn't"—Rita's pencil had paused— "you could tell about how really *dedicated* she is. I mean, with her binoculars and her hat and all, and getting up real early in the morning to go out in the woods or on the lake all by herself. . . ."

Angie's voice trailed off. This didn't sound too fascinating, even to her. She tried again. "I bet she's spent hours hanging around swamps, maybe even *quicksand*, just to get a look at some really special, unusual bird."

But Rita refused to go along with this manufactured drama. "She gets a lot of mosquito bites, that's for sure. And once she sprained her ankle climbing over a rotten log."

"Right," Angie said quickly. "But I bet she didn't make a big deal out of it, did she? Because she's brave—that's one of her main qualities. They like you to put down the person's qualities," she added, and waited while Rita wrote down *"Brave."* "And she has a sense of humor, that's real important. Like the way she laughs at herself about never winning at bingo—"

Angie stopped short as the memory that had chimed faintly a few minutes ago gave off a sudden clang.

"What did you mean, 'lucky in love'?" she demanded. When Rita just gaped at her, she persisted, "That's what you said one night before bingo. You said, 'Unlucky at cards, lucky in love,' and Mrs. Rowan said something about how you might be right, and then she changed the subject. I remember it as clear as day, because that was the night Gus tried to change Mrs. Rowan's luck by switching everyone's bingo cards around, only it didn't work." Angie stood over Rita with her hands on her hips. "So what did you mean?"

Rita looked uncomfortable. "Oh, that was just a joke, sort of. Because of all the stamps."

"Stamps?"

"Yeah. Gran gives me stamps for my collection at home. They come from all over the world, see, and when I asked her where she got them, she said she knew someone that traveled a lot and wrote her letters from a whole bunch of different places. Only she wouldn't tell me who. I did ask her," Rita said defensively, "but she just smiled and said maybe she had a secret admirer."

"Wow, that's *neat*," Angie breathed. She pulled out the chair at the other end of the table and sank into it, gazing unseeingly across the room at a rain-blurred square of window. "A secret admirer. What do you bet it's her long-lost love—the man she would have married if it hadn't been for your grandfather. Wow," she said again, and added with a sigh, "Well, there's your story."

"What is?"

"Your grandmother's tragic life. She was denied her true love, and so she lives alone, thinking sadly of what might have been." Angie didn't know where these words came from, only that they felt right somehow. This must be what people meant by inspiration, she thought in awe.

Rita frowned. "Mostly Gran seems pretty cheerful."

"Because she's brave. You put down 'brave' for one of her qualities, right? Well, there you are." Angie spread her hands. It seemed to her there was nothing more to be said.

"Yeah," Rita said after a pause, "but when did she meet this other guy? I mean, she was married to my grandfather for quite a while, long enough to raise my mom and my Aunt Cecily—that's the twins' mother. And maybe she still is. Married to my grandfather, I mean."

Angie pondered this, but only for a moment. "Well, if it's a *really* long-lost love, maybe she met him before she met your grandfather, back when she was young and glamorous and went to lots of parties and nightclubs and things." Before Rita could object to this unlikely vision of the weatherbeaten Mrs. Rowan, Angie snapped her fingers and exclaimed, "Remember the feather boa? That black scarf thing she let Wanda borrow for the variety show, when Wanda was trying to act out being a bird?"

Rita nodded. It was a scene no one was likely to forget.

"Well, that's *exactly* the kind of thing you'd wear to

a nightclub, right? So it all fits. She fell in love with this handsome man, and they'd dance until dawn and drink champagne and— Come on, Rita, you should be writing all this down."

Rita started to, then stopped and said, "But if she loved this other guy, why didn't she marry him instead of my grandfather?"

"Maybe he was already married," Angie said, thinking of a TV soap opera she sometimes watched when she was home sick from school, "and by the time he was free, she wasn't." Somehow this didn't seem very satisfactory. "Or I know," she said, electrified by a new idea that seemed to have been lurking around a corner of her mind, just waiting for her to pounce on it. "Maybe they were twins!"

"Who were?"

"Your grandfather and the other guy. Sure, they were identical twins! And she married the wrong one by mistake."

Rita had her mulish look again. "I never heard of my grandfather having a twin," she objected.

Angie sighed. "Rita, you barely *know* anything about your grandfather, right? And if there was a what-d'you-call-it, a scandal, they would have hushed it up." She wasn't quite sure who she meant by "they" or just what the scandal would have been, but never mind—it would come to her. "I mean, the whole point of this deal is it's a *mystery*. And with twins in your family—"

Rita said, "I'm pretty sure it's my uncle's family that has twins in it, not my aunt's."

But Angie was on too much of a roll now to be sidetracked by petty details. "Well, probably twins can just happen," she said. "I mean, they have to start somewhere, right? Come on, Rita, if you keep interrupting, you're gonna wreck the whole story."

"But what if it isn't true?"

Angie sat back with a sigh. Some collaborator Rita was turning out to be. "Look, it *could* be true, right?" Rita nodded uncertainly. "And even if it isn't, your teachers out in Colorado aren't going to know the difference." Rita nodded again, looking slightly cheered. "So okay," Angie said briskly, "the first thing to do is write down a title."

"I already have a title," Rita pointed out, consulting her pad. " 'The Most Fascinating Character I Ever Met.' " Except I'm not sure I spelled 'fascinating' right."

"No, no," Angie said. "Scrap that. Here's your title." As she paused for effect, a bell pealed in the distance—a real bell this time, the one announcing breakfast at the lodge. " 'My Grandmother's Tragic Life.' You got that?"

Angie pushed back her chair, looked around for her rain jacket, and remembered she'd decided she wouldn't need it. "I have to go now, but we should be able to finish this up tomorrow morning. I'll probably have some more ideas by then. And then you can pay me."

She left Rita writing laboriously. As she sped along the path in the rain, coins jingling pleasantly in her pocket, Angie thought there was nothing like imagination for working up an appetite. When she encountered Mrs. Rowan coming the other way, trudging along with her hat crammed down over her ears, Angie just nodded at her absently. The actual Mrs. Rowan no longer seemed to have much connection with the fascinating, star-crossed young lover of Angie's creation.

Chapter

✳ ✳ ✳

An hour later, fortified by French toast, sausage patties, and two glasses of chocolate milk, Angie was trying to decide between working on the new jigsaw puzzle in the lounge and playing shuffleboard in the rec house with Sally North. The puzzle was tempting, since someone had already put in all the corners and most of the edges. On the other hand, it was rare for Sally to want to do anything as energetic as shuffleboard, so maybe she shouldn't let the opportunity pass.

"Okay," she told Sally. "Except I think Wanda's in the rec room practicing the piano." Wanda had recently started taking piano lessons from her father, who often played for the Sunday night sings and who'd found an old exercise book inside the piano bench. "She never practices very long, though, in case that tunnel thing starts happening to her hands."

"Carpal tunnel syndrome," Sally supplied. She knew about medical things from her father, who was a doctor. "But anyway, I didn't mean *now*." She gave one of her catlike yawns and pulled down her rain parka from the row of hooks beside the veranda door. "Right now I think I'll go back to bed for a while. It's such a perfect morning for sleeping."

"I can never go back to sleep once I'm up," Angie said, though she found herself yawning too. "When do you want to play shuffleboard, then?"

"Oh, maybe before lunch," Sally said vaguely. She drew the hood of the parka up over her long, honey-colored hair, said, "I'll let you know, okay?" and pushed out the screen door into the drizzle.

Angie turned back into the big, high-raftered room, where a small fire flickered in the blackened hearth, more for cheer than for warmth, since the air was mild. A pleasant hum of conversation and the clink of china came from the dining room beyond the double sets of glass doors, but so far there was no one else in the lounge itself.

She should stake her place at the puzzle table right now, Angie thought. Otherwise it would be taken over by a bunch of the older guests as soon as they finished reading their newspapers and drinking their extra cups of coffee. Angie loved working on a jigsaw puzzle before you could tell what it was going to be about. The rule at Potter's was that no one ever looked at the picture on the cover of the box—in fact Nora usually kept the box in the office safe until the puzzle was done. Once you figured out it was a moose standing in a forest with some foxes and rabbits running around and a mountain in the background, Angie couldn't see taking hours to fill the whole thing in, right down to the missing last piece someone would find under a corner of the rug.

But she hesitated. Something was nagging at her. As she started across the room, she realized what it was— the $7.42 in her jeans pocket, a chunky little weight that gave off a faint clink each time she moved. It wasn't burning a hole in her pocket so much as threatening to go right through it.

Angie sighed, knowing she'd enjoy working on the puzzle a lot more if she put the money safely in the cashbox first. If she cut around behind the lower row of cabins instead of using the path, it shouldn't take her more than three minutes to get up to Cedar Waxwing and back. While she was there, she could also change her T-shirt, which was still damp from her dash to breakfast from Mrs. Rowan's cabin.

With a last look over her shoulder to make sure no one was advancing on the puzzle table, Angie hurried to the side door, gathered herself for a leap off the porch steps into the rain, and almost fell over Hugh Curtis.

He was sitting on the lower step, enveloped in the

oversized, shiny yellow slicker that Rita had once observed made him look like a banana slug. Angie had to take this on faith, since she'd never seen a banana slug. Given Rita's literal mind, though, she figured the description couldn't be far off.

"What are you doing here?" she demanded, grabbing at the railing to steady herself. "For gosh sakes, Hugh, don't you even know enough to come in out of the rain?"

"I was waiting for you," Hugh said, and stood up. The slicker looked even bulkier than usual. In the next moment Angie found out why. "I'm all ready for my lesson," he told her. He tugged at the Velcro closing to show her what he was wearing underneath: his yellow swim trunks, a yellow-and-white striped T-shirt, and a puffy orange life vest.

Angie closed her eyes, hoping Hugh might turn out to be a what-d'you-call-it, a figment of her imagination. She'd forgotten all about the canoe lesson—or more accurately, she'd let herself forget about it accidentally on purpose, on the chance that Hugh might forget too. But when she opened her eyes, he was still there, gazing up at her expectantly.

"It's raining," she said weakly.

"Not hard. And anyway, I've got my slicker."

Angie regarded him with despair. "Hugh, you can't paddle a canoe with a slicker on! Well, maybe someone else could. *I* probably could, but not you."

Hugh accepted this humbly. "Okay. I guess I don't mind getting wet. And you're already wet," he pointed out.

"Because of standing here talking to you," Angie said crossly, moving back under the shelter of the porch roof.

"You promised," Hugh reminded her. "And if you don't keep your promise—"

"Okay, okay!" Angie thought hard. "Here's what we'll do. Now listen to me, Hugh, so you don't get it wrong. I'll meet you up at the end of the lake in a half hour— you know, on past Mrs. Rowan's, just before the road straightens out again. There's a little path there that goes down into the reeds. You wait for me there, where no one can see you, and I'll bring the canoe."

She pictured Hugh plodding along the road past all the cabins and added, "And you don't need to have a life jacket on yet. I'll bring one with me."

Obediently Hugh shrugged out of his slicker and yanked the vest off with a loud, ripping sound—it too had a Velcro closing, being one of the newer ones from the locker farther along the veranda. Angie winced and looked around, but the only people in earshot were the two little kids she'd tried to baby-sit, Jonathan and Miranda, playing some game with an umbrella on the small porch of Tree Swallow nearby.

"A whole half hour," Hugh said disconsolately as Angie took the vest from him. "What am I going to do in the meantime?"

Angie sighed. "Hugh, it'll take you about fifteen minutes just to get there." When he didn't say anything, she said, "Did you have breakfast?"

He shook his head. "I wasn't hungry. I guess I'm sort of nervous."

A moment ago Angie had been wishing for a handful of salt, on the chance that if she threw it at Hugh, he'd turn inside out the way Rita said banana slugs did *(yuck)* when you sprinkled salt on them. Now, meeting his solemn brown eyes, she found herself feeling almost sorry for him. She was about to suggest that he go get a muffin from the basket next to the coffee warmer when there was a piercing scream from Tree Swallow.

They both turned and squinted through the rain. Miranda was clutching her midriff while Jonathan danced around her, brandishing the closed umbrella in one hand and a damp beach towel in the other. Clearly he was the bullfighter and Miranda was the bull. At least he hadn't drawn blood yet, as far as Angie could see. Both children were still in their pajamas.

"Why don't you go over and play with those kids before they hurt each other?" she said to Hugh. This sounded like a dumb question, even to her. "Their mother's probably busy with the baby," she added lamely. "I mean, you wouldn't have to play with them *long*."

To her surprise Hugh nodded thoughtfully. "Yeah," he said. "I guess they'll be glad when their dad finally gets here." Jonathan had Miranda pinned against the railing now, but she'd turned around, and Jonathan evidently considered it unsporting to stab a bull in the back. "He's flying up tomorrow," Hugh went on. "To Burlington, I guess, and then he'll drive. I hope it won't be bad weather for flying. You know, like a lot of fog, so the pilot can't see."

Angie shrugged impatiently. She certainly wasn't going to stand around talking to Hugh Curtis about the weather, of all boring subjects—and weather that wasn't even happening here but way over in Burlington. She said, "I have some stuff I need to do back at the cabin before I get the canoe. Do you have a watch?"

Hugh nodded. "I wear it around my ankle, so I won't forget to take it off when I go swimming."

Angie looked down at Hugh's wet socks and muddy sneakers. They appeared too big for him, like everything else he wore, as if his parents (or his aunt and uncle?) never looked at him long enough to see what size he really was. An ankle didn't strike her as a very convenient place to wear a watch, but at least this explained why Hugh was given to bending double at odd moments, as if seized by sudden cramps.

Miranda had climbed up onto the railing and was clinging to one of the roof supports.

Hugh put his slicker back on. "Okay," he said, "I'll

meet you in a half hour. I know a good game to play with an umbrella," he added. "You open it up and spin it around, and then you see how many times you can run around it before it stops." This didn't sound like much fun to Angie, especially in the confined space of Tree Swallow's front porch, but probably Jonathan and Miranda would think it was great.

As Hugh trudged off, she hastened along the veranda and tossed the life vest into the locker on top of a pile of badminton rackets and boat cushions. When she came back for the paddles, she'd pick out an older vest for Hugh, one that wasn't such a bright, noticeable shade of orange.

Chapter

✳ ✳ ✳

Angie had been right in thinking that the upper part of Heron Lake would be a private place for a canoe lesson. The shoreline around the cove she'd chosen was thick with bushes and small trees, including willows that trailed their fronds on the shallow water.

What she'd forgotten to take into account were the reeds, the water lilies, the mud, and the mosquitoes. Though as Hugh said, the last two sort of went together, since a layer of mud made a good insect repellent once you got it thick enough. This was after he'd fallen overboard several times in an attempt to yank his paddle free of that same mud.

"Don't pull, push!" Angie told him, having given up on "Don't stand up!" But Hugh didn't seem to know the difference between "push" and "pull," any more than he knew his left from his right.

"Usually I can tell them apart from my socks," he said seriously. "I wear a light-color sock on one foot for 'left' and a dark-color sock for 'right.'" This explained another of Hugh's peculiarities—the fact that his socks rarely matched (except of course when he was wearing whites for tennis).

Without much hope, Angie suggested that he try thinking "port" and "starboard" instead, and explained which was which. To her surprise, the new words took.

"Starboard," Hugh repeated, turning his head to beam at Angie, where she stood slapping at mosquitoes in knee-deep water—she'd long since given up trying to stay in the canoe with him. "That's easy, because if I want to see the stars at night, my window is on the right—at least I'm pretty sure it's the right." He gestured, and Angie nodded, watching the canoe rock dangerously. "And the wall is made of *boards*, see? Of course, that's here. It might not work at home."

"Watch the tree," Angie said as the canoe drifted toward a half-submerged limb Hugh had already banged into several times. Luckily she'd thought to bring the most battered of the aluminum canoes instead of one of the good fiberglass ones.

"So if I want to turn to port," Hugh continued, brandishing his paddle, "I just put the oar on the starboard side, right?"

"Right," Angie agreed, slapping at another mosquito. "I mean, yes."

She hadn't even tried to explain backwatering, let alone how to do a sweep that would keep the canoe headed in a straight line. She figured if Hugh could learn to stay afloat while going around in circles, that would be enough for one lesson.

"You should put some more mud on," Hugh called, pushing off from the tree limb with an energy that sent the canoe hissing over a thick bed of yellow water lilies. "Then you won't even feel the mosquitoes."

What she should have put on, Angie thought grimly, was a wet suit and a pair of rubber boots. She didn't mind the feeling of muck between her toes, but having it close around her ankles was something else again. She'd found herself beginning to have Wanda-like thoughts about water snakes and snapping turtles, not to mention the possibility of sinking beneath the surface altogether. Since no one but Hugh knew where she was and no one ever listened to Hugh, she could forget about being rescued. "Disappearance at Heron Lake"—now there was a title for Rita.

Hugh was trying to extricate himself from the water lilies, whose stems seemed to have wound themselves around the throat of his paddle. Before Angie could yell at him again not to stand up, he leaned over too far trying to unwind them and overturned the canoe.

This time the splash was muffled by all the lily pads. With a sigh, Angie wrenched one foot and then the other out of the mud and waded over. As Hugh emerged, spluttering and dripping, she helped him right the canoe, then held the sides steady while he clambered back in.

"Gosh, these things are real *tippy*, aren't they?" he said breathlessly. "Now, let's see, what did I do with my paddle? Oh, well, I can always use yours."

The stern paddle, he meant, which was longer and heavier than the bow paddle he'd been using. Angie couldn't even begin to imagine the damage Hugh might inflict with it. At the very least, he was bound to wind up poking himself in the eye with the handle. Hastily she groped around underwater, found the missing paddle, and handed it to him.

"Okay," she said, "one more time around, and that's it."

"You mean the lesson's over?" Hugh's face fell. "What time is it? You said an hour."

"That was only if it stopped raining," Angie said, "and it's starting again." Hugh's watch was over on the bank with his shoes and slicker. Angie didn't want to go look at it, fearing it might really have been only about twenty minutes since she'd paddled into the cove and found Hugh waiting on the bank as directed. "Anyway, you'll need to go change before your aunt and uncle get back from Gilead."

"Oh, they'll just think I've been out in the rain," Hugh assured her, yanking at a reed that had draped itself around his ear. The canoe wobbled, and Angie grabbed its side. "But okay, I guess I might have had enough practice for now. I'm using new muscles and everything, and I wouldn't want to be sore for my next lesson." Angie closed her eyes. Had she really promised three lessons? "Also, I think I'm really getting the hang of it. Now, which way should I go this time, port or starboard?"

"Starboard," Angie said, eyeing the water lilies and the submerged tree. "And don't try to sit up on the seat—just kneel on the bottom, right in the middle, like I showed you. That way maybe you won't fall in again."

Hugh's last ducking had washed off most of the mud. In his striped shirt and yellow swim trunks, he looked like a sodden bee wearing a faded safety vest, Angie thought, fighting off an attack of giggles. Except that a bee would have more control over its elbows, if bees had elbows.

Hugh spun the canoe around violently, then had to brake by stabbing his paddle into the mud. At least the paddle didn't get stuck this time, nor did the impact tumble him over the side. Frowning in concentration and breathing rapidly through his nose, he eased the bow into a slower, wider circle. "Oh, wow," he said. "This is the best I've done yet."

"Don't talk," Angie commanded. "And don't look around."

She was pleased in spite of herself to see that Hugh had achieved a measure of control over the canoe, even if all he was doing was paddling gingerly around in a circle. She stood watching with her arms folded while the increasing rain plastered her hair to the sides of her head. There was no way she could get any wetter, and at least the rain had driven the mosquitoes under cover. When the canoe had completed another full circle, she waded forward, grabbed the bow, and pulled it toward shore.

"Can't I go around one more time?" Hugh pleaded.

"No," Angie said firmly. "You should quit while you're ahead." Somehow she felt this might be especially important in Hugh's case, not because he'd get down on himself—that seemed impossible—but because some kind of muscle memory might carry over to the next lesson.

She helped him out of the canoe so he wouldn't trip over the strut and go sprawling in the mud again, and waited while he gathered up his gear and handed her the life vest.

"You better go take a hot shower," she directed, noticing that his teeth were chattering. "And if you meet anyone on the way, just say you were down here catching frogs or something." Hugh nodded solemnly and plodded off through the reeds.

With a groan of relief, Angie shoved the canoe away from shore, hopped aboard, and picked up her paddle.

She hadn't taken more than five or six strokes when an unwelcome sight met her eyes—her cousin Gus, fishing from the bank of the next cove, beyond a clump of willows that had screened him from view. He was wearing his waders, a rubber poncho, and an expression of contained mirth.

"How long have you been here?" Angie said in dismay, digging her paddle in to stop the canoe while keeping a wary eye out for Gus's fishing line.

"Oh, for more or less the whole lesson, I guess." Gus let out the strangled-sounding snort that meant he was laughing. "What were you doing, anyway—teaching him to punt?"

"Punt?" Angie echoed, thinking of football.

"Like they do in England." Gus snorted again. Angie waited for him to explain the joke, the way you often had to with Gus. "They have these flat-bottom boats that they take out on these muddy little rivers, only instead of rowing or paddling, they push them along with a pole. They have to stand up to do it. Except I guess they don't fall overboard as often as Hugh Curtis. Anyway"—he reeled in his line, inspected the gross-looking purple plastic worm on the end of it, and cast again past Angie's shoulder— "if Hugh can't learn to paddle a canoe, I'd say the next best thing would be to ship him over to England."

Angie could think of no suitable retort to this, being too preoccupied with figuring out what she could offer Gus to keep his mouth shut. Still, she felt she should defend Hugh somehow. "At least he was trying," she said lamely.

"Yeah—trying too hard, as usual. But I guess if anyone can teach him, it's you." As Angie stared at him in surprise, Gus said with a shrug, "I don't know why you'd want to bother in the first place, but you were real patient with him, you know? If it'd been me, I would've been yelling and screaming and throwing stuff at him—either that or busting out laughing. But you acted like he really *could* learn."

This was one of the few compliments Angie had ever received from Gus—if it really was a compliment, she thought uncertainly. He might mean that only she would be dumb enough to think Hugh Curtis could ever learn to paddle a canoe. She settled for saying, "Yeah, well, I don't like people yelling and screaming at me, either, when I'm trying to learn something. So I guess that's why."

"Right," Gus said, giving his line an experimental tug, then reeling in again.

Angie cleared her throat and gave her head the little toss she used whenever she was about to say something important. Usually her hair tossed with it, but today it was slicked down by rain.

"Listen, Gus, what you said about laughing . . . I guess Steve doesn't have to know about this, does he?" Steve was the only person Gus would be likely to tell about the canoe lesson. Unfortunately, Steve would also be the very worst person he could tell.

"About what?" Gus was busy replacing the purple

worm with a shocking-pink crayfish. "Oh. No, why would he? He thinks Hugh Curtis is a dweeb, anyway. Darn, this thing's losing one of its legs."

Angie realized thankfully that she and Hugh had been only an interlude in Gus's ongoing mission to hook a bass out of Heron Lake on a rainy day. Her spirits lifting, she thrust her paddle into the water and skimmed off toward the distant dock. She'd take a hot shower herself, she decided, and maybe put on her new red T-shirt, since Rita didn't want it. By then Sally might be awake again and ready to play shuffleboard.

Chapter

✳ ✳ ✳

The stamps?" said Rita. "Why do you want to see the stamps?"

"Because they might give me some new ideas."

It was the next morning, and Angie was buttering a piece of toast in Mrs. Rowan's sunny kitchen. She'd persuaded Rita that her imagination worked even better on a full stomach.

Rita frowned, standing in the doorway with her spiral pad. "I don't think I need any more *new* ideas. I just need to know which ones to save and which ones to cross out."

"That's because we still haven't figured out the whole story," Angie said, and added, "Where do you keep the jam?"

"But if there aren't going to be any twins—"

"Oh, there'll still be twins," Angie assured her. "The

tragedy's gonna be that your grandmother chose the wrong one." She found a jar of currant jelly in a cupboard. "Go get the stamps, okay?"

Angie had abandoned the idea of mistaken identity as being too farfetched, even for a story. Surely Mrs. Rowan—even a young, giddy Mrs. Rowan, exhausted from dancing in nightclubs till dawn—would have noticed some difference between her twin boyfriends, even if it was just the way they did the tango or the waltz or whatever people danced to in those days.

No, what she'd done was marry the steady, reliable twin, when all along it was really the charming, madcap adventurer she loved. Or maybe it was the other way around. Angie hadn't quite made up her mind.

There were more stamps than Angie had expected, and as Rita said, they came from all over the world. She dumped them out of an envelope onto the table, and Angie studied them while she ate her toast.

"The adventurer," she decided aloud. "I can't see the nice, boring one traveling around this much, can you? Especially now, when he'd be pretty old. Unless . . ." She paused, licked butter from her index finger, and slid several of the stamps closer. "Indonesia," she said in a hushed voice. "Chile. Iceland—that's way up north somewhere." She stared at Rita. "Wow. Don't you see what this means?"

"What?" said Rita nervously, her pencil poised. "I'm not too good on geography," she confessed.

"I am," Angie told her. "My school makes a big deal about it." She was cheered by the thought that she'd actually found an interesting use for all those tedious hours spent memorizing maps. "See, these are really far-out places — not regular tourist places, I mean."

"So?"

"So they're the kind of places you might go if you were hiding out from someone. If you were a what-d'you-call-it, a *fugitive*." Angie sank back in her chair. "Sure. That's it. That must be it!"

"There are stamps from regular places, too," Rita pointed out. "Look, there's France and Italy."

She pushed these toward Angie, but Angie ignored them. "What I think is, one of them did away with the other."

"Did away with—?"

"Killed," Angie said impatiently. "One twin killed the other."

Rita wrote this down, but said, "Why?"

"For love of your grandmother. That's what this whole deal is about, remember? Tragic, star-crossed love."

"Well, it sure didn't work out, then," Rita objected. "I mean, it's not like he got to be *with* her. All he gets to do is travel around the world hiding out from the cops."

Angie thought about this. "Maybe he thought he could make the murder look like an accident. Or maybe he didn't care. If *he* couldn't have her, he'd make sure his brother couldn't either." She finished her last corner of toast. "That makes it even more tragic."

Rita looked confused. "Which twin was my grandfather, then? And when did all this happen? Because my grandfather was around long enough to have a family and do a job and everything."

Angie was feeling a little confused herself, but she wasn't about to say so. She said experimentally, "He might not have been *home* all that time, though. He might have been in prison. That would explain why your family never talks about him. I mean, talk about a scandal!"

"My mom talks about him sometimes," Rita objected. "It's just I never really listened."

"Or maybe neither of the twins was your grandfather," Angie said with a shrug, scratching at a mosquito bite. Somehow she couldn't get back in the zone today. It was a beautiful morning, and she was supposed to go horseback riding later on, only she'd forgotten to bring her hard hat this year and she needed to ask Wanda if she could borrow hers.

"Maybe there *weren't* any twins," she went on recklessly. "Maybe your grandfather is just—well, whoever he is, and your grandmother got divorced from him, and meanwhile this other guy that writes all the letters is just a secret admirer, like she said."

But Rita didn't seem to be listening. She was thumbing back through the messy pages of her spiral pad, muttering to herself. "If he already went to prison," she said, "why would he still be a fugitive now?" She chewed on her lower lip for a moment. "I know— maybe he escaped!"

"Right," Angie said encouragingly. She remembered she'd never set a time for Hugh's next canoe lesson. Would he be expecting one this morning? Maybe she should stop off on her way to breakfast and tell him they'd have to wait till the afternoon, because of riding. She didn't want him hanging around in his bathing suit, pestering her, in case someone noticed.

"Those old pictures," Rita said. She flopped back in her chair and gazed round-eyed at Angie. "The ones I told you about, with the rocks and the water and everything. Do you think . . . could he have been in one of those really *scary* prisons, like Alcatraz or Devil's Island?"

"I don't see why not," Angie told her.

"Wow. That'd be some escape! Hey, what are you doing?"

Angie had begun scooping the stamps back into their envelope, whose own stamp, she noticed, had been carefully removed. It was addressed in an angular, sloping hand to Mrs. Miriam Rowan, c/o Potter's Lodge and Family Camp. There was no return address. "Well, hey, you don't need me anymore," she pointed out. "Not now that you're starting to have ideas of your own."

Rita looked dazed. "Yeah, I am, aren't I? Of course, I

haven't really started *writing* yet, but . . ." She turned to a fresh page and picked up her pencil. "You know, I just realized the guy in the pictures might not be my grandfather at all. It could be his twin brother, the bad guy, only my mom wouldn't know the difference. Or if she did . . . " She broke off with a frown as Angie edged toward the doorway and the fresh, sweet-smelling morning beyond.

"That's okay," Angie said quickly. "You can pay me later."

"No, it's just my pencil needs sharpening again."

As Rita looked around for her Swiss Army knife— the same knife she used for whittling—Angie backed onto the porch, closed the screen door softly so as not to interrupt Rita's concentration, and skimmed down the steps. The remaining $7.42 was as good as in the bank, she thought jubilantly. Now all she had left to deal with was Hugh Curtis.

Chapter

✻ ✻ ✻

Angie was halfway up the steep path to Loon, the medium-sized cabin occupied by the Curtises, before it occurred to her that it might be a bit early to pay someone a visit. The breakfast bell hadn't even rung yet.

Well, if no one was up, she could always sneak around and tap on Hugh's window. She knew which one it was because her own family had been stuck in Loon the first few years they'd come to Potter's, and she and Steve had had to share the small back bedroom with the bunk beds in it. They'd spent most of their time fighting about who got to have the upper bunk, even though on hot nights you could hardly breathe up there near the ceiling.

But Mrs. Curtis was already up and dressed. Angie could see her through the screen door, wearing one of her interchangeable pastel shirt-dresses and matching canvas shoes. As Angie crossed the porch, she rose from the armchair where she'd been doing needlework and put a finger to her lips. At the same moment, there was a violent sneeze from the back of the cabin.

"Oh, dear, I was hoping he'd gone back to sleep," Mrs. Curtis said, holding the door open for Angie. There was a look of dismay on her soft, powdered features. "Such a *noisy* cold, and my poor husband does need his rest."

It took Angie a moment to work out that it was Hugh who had the cold, even though Mrs. Curtis seemed more concerned about her husband. But maybe not, because in the next instant, Mrs. Curtis said, "I don't think Hugh has a fever, but I didn't want to bother him with the thermometer. He has such trouble keeping still, you know."

Angie hid a grin. She couldn't imagine Hugh holding a thermometer in his mouth for a whole three minutes without either swallowing it or biting it in two.

"And I believe his throat hurts," Mrs. Curtis went on, wincing at another volley of sneezes from the back room. "Some hot tea, I thought, as soon as the dining room opens . . . or I suppose ginger ale would be better for a child, without the caffeine. . . . Oh, I do hope it's not the flu." She gazed distractedly through the side window at the cabin next door. "So comforting, having Dr. North nearby, though it seems a shame to bother him when he's on vacation."

"It's probably just that same cold that's been going around," Angie told her, torn between sympathy for Hugh and joy at the thought of not having to give him another canoe lesson, at least not today. "My aunt has it too."

"Oh, of course," Mrs. Curtis said, looking relieved. "It's so difficult, you know, never having had children of our own. We do our best with Hugh, but I'm afraid we mostly just let him go his own way. Luckily, he's an independent little boy, always busy with some project or other." Angie nodded politely, though "independent" wasn't exactly the word she would have chosen for Hugh. "And as long as he stays healthy and doesn't do anything foolish—"

Hugh was coughing now, in a way that made Angie's own throat hurt. She wondered if she should feel guilty about letting him get so wet yesterday. No, she decided. For one thing, you got a cold from a virus, and for another, how could she have stopped him?

But Mrs. Curtis no longer seemed to be listening. She consulted her watch, crossed the room to the door of the main bedroom, and said brightly, "Rise and shine, Alfred! It's our day for the flea market, remember, and we want to get a good start." The Curtises were always going off antiquing in back-country towns, though they never seemed to buy anything. To Angie she said a little defensively, "I'm sure Nora won't mind looking in on Hugh during the day, and of course I'll give him an aspirin before we leave. Now, what was it you wanted, dear?"

Angie found herself thinking that what Hugh needed right now was a glass of water and a hug, the kind her mother would have bestowed on her automatically, but of course she couldn't say so. And of course she couldn't mention the canoe lesson Hugh wasn't going to be having.

She said, "Oh, I just had something to tell Hugh, but that's okay. I'll catch him later." She turned to go. Somehow, though, she couldn't make herself open the door. A question was lodged in her mind like a splinter. She turned back to Mrs. Curtis and said, "What happened to Hugh's parents?"

Mrs. Curtis looked surprised. "Why, they were killed in a plane crash several years ago. I thought most people knew. I'm sure I must have mentioned it to your parents."

Angie realized to her shame that she'd never thought to ask her parents anything about Hugh. He was just Hugh the dweeb, good for a laugh or two, not worth anyone's serious thought.

Mrs. Curtis was frowning. "You mean Hugh never talks about them?"

Angie shook her head. She said, "Was there a storm? Is that why the plane went down?"

"No, dear, it was fog—a terrible fog over the Great Lakes in the middle of winter, which meant there was ice as well. They think it must have affected the instruments and caused the plane to stall." She bowed her head sadly. "I'm sorry to say they never recovered most of the bodies, including those of Hugh's parents."

Angie stared at her. The breakfast bell was clanging, and Hugh was sneezing again. Wordlessly, she pushed through the door and descended the steps to the path.

She remembered Hugh's worry about the father of the Tree Swallow family, and prayed that he'd arrive safely tonight for everyone's sake, including Hugh's. Her eyes smarting, Angie looked down at the blue dazzle of Heron Lake in the morning sunlight. You certainly couldn't ask for better flying weather, she thought. It was a perfect summer day, without a cloud in the sky— and not a hint of fog.

Chapter

✳ ✳ ✳

A ngie, could you give me a hand with these things?
They're so darned heavy, and I need to clean
behind them."

Nora was dusting and reorganizing the lower
bookshelves in the lounge, behind the puzzle table.
Angie had been studying the puzzle without much
interest—it was almost complete, missing only the tail
feathers of several hawks—while she waited for Wanda
to come by with her riding hat.

"Sure," she said, and almost staggered under the
weight of the two large, leather-bound volumes Nora
piled into her arms. "What are these, anyway?" she
asked as she lowered them onto a nearby bench.

"Oh, some ancient photograph albums. No one ever
throws anything away around here, in case you hadn't
noticed." Nora straightened and ran a hand through her

short dark hair, leaving a smudge on one temple. Her vivid blue eyes were bright with irritation. "Beth was supposed to help me with this job after she got through with the upper cabins, but she hasn't even arrived yet. Either her cold's worse"—she grunted, heaving out another album and blowing dust from the cover— "or her boyfriend's overslept again. Still, you'd think she'd at least have the courtesy to call."

Angie nodded absently, turning over the brittle pages of the topmost album. She smiled at a faded photo of a bunch of dressed-up people going for what appeared to be a hayride—at least, they were sitting in a big pile of straw that had a pair of rickety-looking wheels beneath it. "Look at the hats!" she said.

Nora leaned over to take a look. "Before my time," she remarked with a grin, and added, "Thank heaven. What a lot of work those hayrides must have been, especially afterward, for the girls in the laundry. They had five girls working at a time, so I've been told." These days Potter's made do with Yvette, the wife of Hal the handyman, who washed the sheets and towels at her home in West Eliot, along with some of the guests' laundry. Since Yvette's prices were pretty steep, most people who stayed for any length of time used the Laundromat over in Gilead.

Angie opened the volume Nora had just added to the pile and immediately jumped forward forty years or so—to the 1950s, she thought vaguely, studying the women's Bermuda shorts and pageboy hairstyles.

"Hi, Angie," said a voice at her elbow. It was Wanda, who'd come silently in the side door. Wanda always moved quietly, as if she feared stirring up dust motes that might have germs in them, or perhaps awakening a stray copperhead dozing in a corner.

"I hope this hat is okay. It's my extra one," she explained, as Angie looked at the identical black hard hat on Wanda's head. "I decided to go riding today too," she said shyly. "Since it's so, well, *calm* out. And also it won't be crowded, because there's hardly anyone signed up."

At any other time Angie would have asked Wanda why she needed two hard hats, considering she went horseback riding only once or twice during her vacation—cautiously and slowly, on the fattest and laziest of the horses.

But as she took the hat from Wanda, Angie's gaze fell on a snapshot of a family group posed on the rocks at Great Harriman. It was a familiar setting, with the boathouse in the background (but not the annex—that must have been built later). One of the faces looked vaguely familiar too. But it was the caption under the photo that riveted Angie's attention, even though all it said was *"The Gang's All Here!"*—the kind of cheerful, silly thing people were always writing on snapshots. She stared at the family: a mother and father and two little girls. . . .

"Angie?" Wanda cleared her throat. "I think it's time we went over to the stables. So we can help Karen with the saddles and everything."

Angie closed the album slowly, her thoughts in a whirl. She'd told herself she was through with the whole confusing story, but this—

"Sometimes it takes me extra time with Butterscotch," Wanda was explaining earnestly. "He always puffs himself up when I try to do the girth. Karen says to punch him in the stomach, but that seems kind of mean. Besides, it might make him mad, and what if he tried to kick me or bite me? Still, I wouldn't want the saddle to slip when we're going fast, like trotting or something. . . ."

* * *

Belly Dancer hadn't been ridden in several days and was bursting with energy on this fresh, sunny morning. Since Angie was bursting with the discovery she'd just made, the combination made for a messy departure from the stable yard.

"Shorten up on those reins, Angie," Karen yelled as Belly Dancer plunged toward the long, tin-roofed structure that served as a car shed, then spun around, snorting.

"I thought we'd be going in the woods today," Wanda said. As usual she was bringing up the rear, behind two teenage sisters, Molly and Dana something, who made up the rest of the party.

"Things are still pretty wet from yesterday," Karen told her, leading them toward the corner of the lodge. "I figured we'd hit the open road instead."

Angie tightened her knees, sat up straight, and persuaded Belly Dancer to settle into a reasonably sedate walk. She grinned to herself at the dismay in Wanda's voice. Unlike the narrow woods trails, the open road—by which Karen meant the dirt road to the head of Heron Lake, then the fork that had once been a back road to Gilead—offered plenty of places to let the horses run.

They filed along below the veranda. Karen reined in her big roan to speak to someone sitting in one of the rockers there, and Angie leaned down to adjust a stirrup. One reason she disliked saddling her own horse was that she always seemed to count the stirrup holes wrong and wind up with one foot higher than the other. She straightened up in time to see Rita leaving the veranda at the far end, a can of soda in her hand. She must have just finished her archery practice.

Angie rode Belly Dancer around Karen's horse.

"Rita!" she said in a stage whisper as Rita turned onto the cabin path. Startled, Rita swung around. "Have you started writing the story yet?" Rita nodded. "Well, don't do any more!"

Karen called sharply, "Angie, please stay in line."

"Listen, I can't talk now," Angie said unnecessarily

as Belly Dancer tossed her head and backed away from a butterfly investigating the petunias planted around the flagpole. "When can I see you?"

Rita considered, keeping her distance. She talked a lot about riding what she called cow ponies at home, but here at Potter's she didn't seem to ride much more than Wanda did. She said the one Western saddle was too big for her and that the horses didn't know how to neck-rein, whatever that was.

"After lunch, I guess," she said. "Gran's going over to Yvette's then, to get her hair done." In addition to doing laundry, Yvette did ladies' hair in her kitchen. "How about two o'clock?" She had to raise her voice because of a growing mechanical sputter and roar in the distance.

Angie nodded, and turned Belly Dancer back toward the road. Karen had ridden forward, but the other riders were bunched up by the veranda. The two sisters were talking and giggling about something, while Wanda had edged Butterscotch up alongside them because of a car behind her—Dr. North, waiting patiently for the horses to get out of the way so he could go play golf in Canada.

"Okay, gang," Karen called over her shoulder. "Let's get this show on the road."

She got more of a show than she'd bargained for. They all did. Wanda said later it wasn't Angie's fault, but Angie felt guiltily that if she'd been paying more attention, instead of thinking about what she had to tell Rita, she could have prevented Belly Dancer's startled leap across the road as the mechanical noise she'd been hearing resolved itself into an approaching motorcycle—Beth, arriving late for work.

As it was, Angie started a chain reaction, with Butterscotch at the end of the chain. Normally the least spookable of horses, he must have felt hemmed in between the car nosing at his heels and all the activity up ahead. Whatever the reason, he bolted onto the grass beside the driveway and galloped down onto the tennis court (fortunately unoccupied at the time), where he jumped over the net and skidded to a halt inches from the fence at the far end.

"That's right," Karen yelled to Wanda, "ride him into a corner."

But Wanda wasn't riding Butterscotch so much as hanging on to him. Before she could clutch at the reins, he turned and cantered back along the fence and up onto the grass. There he shied at the big oak tree as if he'd never seen a tree before, and took off up the road.

Angie meanwhile was having her own troubles with Belly Dancer, whose leap had carried them onto the badminton lawn beyond the tennis court. She was just hauling the mare's head around, trying to avoid trampling a bed of zinnias, when Butterscotch thundered by with Wanda clinging to his neck.

"If you catch up first," Karen yelled, busy with the other two horses, "try to grab the bridle."

Angie hadn't realized she was trying to catch up, but Belly Dancer had already made this decision for her. The mare shot off after Butterscotch's shiny blond rump like a thoroughbred leaving the starting gate. The sight of the motorcycle at the side of the road—Angie had a fleeting glimpse of Beth standing next to it with her hands over her mouth—only seemed to spur her on.

Instinctively Angie leaned forward, relaxed her elbows, and clamped hard with her knees. Wow! This was the fastest she'd ever gone on a horse, she thought, as cabins and trees whipped by in a brown-green blur on her left and the lake become a streak of blue on her right. She tried not to notice that she was being run away with almost as much as Wanda was. She also tried not to think about encountering Wanda's dead body around the next curve in the road.

"Grab the bridle," Karen had said. That sounded kind of tricky, at a full gallop. Or had she said "*Don't* grab the bridle"? But never mind. Right now Angie needed all of her concentration just to stay in the saddle as Belly Dancer hurtled into the big curve . . .

. . . and overran the other pair by a good fifty yards, the distance it took Angie to rein Belly Dancer to a halt and get turned around. Butterscotch was cropping grass at the side of the road, his flanks heaving. Wanda stood next to him, brushing off her hat.

"Are you okay?" Angie called breathlessly, riding back through her own dust.

Wanda nodded. "He just stopped," she said, looking at Butterscotch. "I think he got tired all of a sudden." Angie grinned—this must have been the farthest Butterscotch had run in years, not to mention the fastest. "And then I fell off. Well, I sort of slid off." Wanda looked a little shaken, but her eyes were shining. "It wasn't nearly as bad as I thought."

"What wasn't?" Angie saw Karen coming around the curve at a gallop, trailed by the other two riders, and waved to show her everything was all right.

"Having a horse run away with me." Wanda put her hat back on and patted Butterscotch's sweaty neck, gazing at him in something like awe. "Did you see him jump over the tennis net? I didn't even know he could jump. Sometimes he won't even step over a log—he has to go around it instead."

Angie was trying to keep Belly Dancer from eating a large purple thistle. She felt trembly all of a sudden, and wouldn't have minded heading straight back to the stables. But Wanda was fastening the strap of her hat, gathering up the reins, and leading Butterscotch over to a stump so she could remount. When Karen and the others rode up, she said she and Butterscotch would go last, the way they always did.

"So we don't slow anyone down," she said apologetically, appearing not to notice the lathered flanks of the other four horses. She put one foot up on the stump, then withdrew it with a frown. "Gosh, I hope this stump isn't *rotten* inside. That'd be a good way to break an ankle. . . ."

Chapter

✳ ✳ ✳

I t's funny about Wanda," Angie said to Steve, telling him about the morning's ride back at Cedar Waxwing. "She says things are a whole lot scarier when she's thinking about them than they are when they really happen." She thought for a moment. "She's just the opposite of me."

"That's because you never think more than two minutes ahead," Steve said sourly, wadding up his sandwich wrapper and tossing it accurately into the wastebasket across the room.

Angie opened her mouth and closed it again. If Steve only knew how much thinking ahead she'd had to do lately! But of course that was something she couldn't mention. She looked around and said, "Did you bring me my lunch, too?"

He nodded at the full knapsack lying at the end of

the wicker couch next to his empty one. Angie started to ask him to help her off with her riding boots, but thought better of it. He was in a bad mood because Gus had gone waterskiing with some people who had a cottage over on Great Harriman—Gus, who normally had no use for power boats in any form, because they scared fish, and who'd never even tried waterskiing before. Steve thought the least Gus could have done was get him invited too.

Sure enough, he couldn't resist another dig about the horseback ride. "Hi-Yo, Silver," he drawled. "Angie rides again. Quite the little heroine you're getting to be around here."

Angie hadn't admitted in so many words that her horse had bolted too. Steve would figure that out sooner or later, if he hadn't already. She ignored him, sitting down on the floor to tug at the heel of her left boot and trying to remember what kind of sandwiches she'd ordered today. Now that she'd stopped feeling so shaky, she was starved.

"Read any good books to Mr. Jeffries lately?" Steve went on. "Or better yet"—he lounged back against the couch with his most maddening smile— "seen any good videos?"

Angie froze.

"Come on, Angie, I've known about that loose floorboard for ages. I had that room one year, remember?" He laughed at her expression. "What'd you do with the thing, anyway? Give it away as another good deed? Or throw it in the lake? I mean, geez, *Attack of the Giant Leeches!* That's pretty gross, even for you."

"Leeches?" Angie said before she could stop herself. "Is *that* what those things were?" Her stomach churned, and not just from hunger.

Steve doubled over and slapped his knee. When he could speak again, he said, "It also translates as 'Blood-suckers.' Course, you'd never think of using Mom's French dictionary. Oh, no, that might actually require a few brains. You didn't even notice when I turned the video over, which I did a couple of times just to see if you'd catch on. I mean, talk about Angie the airhead!"

Angie scrambled to her feet and doubled up her fists. "Don't call me that." She remembered she still had her boots on and drew back her foot to deliver a kick.

Before she could land it, Steve held up a hand and said, "Sorry, sorry. I'm sure you have all the brains you're ever gonna need. Anyway, you don't have time for a fight. I forgot to tell you, your pal Rita wants you up at Mrs. Rowan's cabin right now."

"Now?" Angie stared at him, disconcerted. "But I was going to meet her this afternoon." Belatedly, she added, "And she's not my pal."

"Yeah? Then why've you been sneaking up there the last two mornings?" Steve paused to let this latest feat of surveillance sink in, then said, "Rita said it was real important. Of course, with Rita, you never know what that means. She might have gotten a knot in her lasso she needs you to help her undo."

Angie snatched up the nearest thing at hand, which happened to be Wanda's riding hat, hurled it at Steve as hard as she could, and slammed out the door. His "Ow!" of pain wasn't as satisfying as it might have been, considering she was also leaving her lunch behind. Why did she always seem to be dealing with Rita Crawford on an empty stomach?

Fuming, Angie jogged down to the main cabin path, then slowed to a walk as her boots began pinching. Mrs. Rowan's plans must have changed, she decided, if it was so important for them to meet now. Well, at the very least, Rita could help her get her boots off, since Steve never would.

Also, the meeting didn't have to be a long one, she reminded herself. All she really needed to do was give Rita her new piece of information and let her try and make sense of it. Then she'd get paid—which after all was the whole point, never mind what Rita decided to put down in her story. As for the story itself, it couldn't be any dumber than a family of whittled chipmunks.

In this businesslike mood Angie clomped up the porch steps, to find Rita waiting for her just inside the screen door.

"Okay," she said briskly, "here's the deal." Rita was blocking the doorway and making urgent signals about something or other, but Angie refused to be distracted.

"Your grandfather's still alive. Not only that, he's the one that's been sending all those letters to your grandmother. I figured it out from the handwriting."

Rita looked stricken. Angie didn't know what reaction she'd expected, but it wasn't this. Maybe Rita was thinking about all the rewriting she'd have to do.

"Those old photo albums in the lodge," Angie explained. "There's a picture of your grandmother with two little girls—your mother, I guess, and your aunt—and a man that's pretty much got to be your grandfather. He's good-looking," she added, a little rattled by Rita's agonized expression, "but not dashing, like we thought. His legs are kind of skinny. But anyway, it says 'The Gang's All Here' under the picture, and the handwriting is the same as the writing on that envelope, the one you had the stamps in."

"I always thought his legs were rather elegant, myself," said a voice behind Rita.

Angie blinked as Rita ducked aside with a little whimper. It was dim inside the cabin after the brilliant sunshine outside, but there was no mistaking the grim figure of Mrs. Rowan in the middle of the living room, nor what she was holding in her hand—Rita's spiral pad.

"Just what did you think you were doing, Angie?" she demanded.

"Didn't Rita explain?" Angie faltered. "I was helping her with a story for school. Just with the ideas," she added hastily, not wanting to let Rita down any more than she apparently already had.

"Ideas about my private life."

"Well, yes. But they weren't supposed to be *true*, necessarily. I mean, we were just trying to figure stuff out, like you do with a story—you know, making up combinations of things so they'd explain what happened. What might have happened," Angie amended, quailing before the look in Mrs. Rowan's eyes. "And it was mostly me," she confessed. "Not Rita."

"That much I'd gathered," Mrs. Rowan said drily. "I doubt anyone has ever accused Rita of letting her imagination run away with her. Whereas you—" She put on her reading glasses and riffled distastefully through the pages of the notebook. "This isn't just running away, it's *galloping*."

Angie cringed, remembering her recent adventure on Belly Dancer.

"Identical twins, prison escapes, murders, nightclubs . . . nightclubs! I don't think I've been in a nightclub more than twice in my life. And as for doing the tango—"

She gave a sudden snort of laughter and sank down onto the couch. It was on the tip of Angie's tongue to ask about the feather boa, but she decided she'd better not, even though Mrs. Rowan now seemed more amused than angry.

"Oh, dear," she said, removing her glasses and tossing the pad aside. "Angie, you may have a brilliant future in some creative field, but it's *not* going to be in fiction. I never saw a more confused plot in my life. I know, I know, you were still working it out—or poor Rita was—but still . . ."

She leaned back and laughed without restraint. Angie bit her lip. She didn't think the story had been quite that bad, though of course it had needed some smoothing out.

Mrs. Rowan wiped her eyes and said to Rita, who was watching her anxiously, "Get me a handkerchief, would you, dear? Not tissues, a proper handkerchief— you'll find one in my top dresser drawer. And then you can come back and sit down and I'll tell you both the real story of my marriage."

And she proceeded to do so. It was a dramatic story in its way, involving a mining claim (Mr. Rowan, it turned out, was a geologist), a family dispute over money, and a disagreement between husband and wife about how and where to live. It wasn't as tragic as the story Angie had concocted for Rita, but it was almost as sad, though it had its funny side, too.

Unfortunately, it was a story Angie was never going to be able to tell anyone, not even her parents. Because before Mrs. Rowan uttered a word, she swore them both to silence.

Chapter

✳ ✳ ✳

Angie sat brooding on the steps of Cedar Waxwing, huddled in an old hooded sweatshirt of Steve's and her heaviest pair of jeans. The evening had turned unexpectedly cold, and the air was tangy with wood smoke from all the cabin stoves. Inside, her family was playing hearts around the old card table whose short leg had to be propped up with a folded matchbook. Angie had refused to join them, even though hearts was one of her better games. Somehow she found it easy to keep track of all the suits and face cards, including the dreaded queen of spades. She did this in the same automatic way she kept track of money in her head— not really thinking, just counting. It was a trait that maddened Steve.

Money! she thought morosely. Here she'd expected to be all paid up by tonight, and instead she was still

$3.71 short of refilling the cashbox. In fact, Rita had balked at paying her anything at all, pointing out that the story was wrecked and that she was going to have to start all over again on a whole new project. She already had something in mind—making a wreath out of pinecones. If she did a good enough shellac job, she should be able to dust it off later, spray it with glitter, and give it to her mother for a Christmas present.

A loon gave its crazy-sounding laugh in the distance. Angie thought bitterly that she should have known better than to get involved with a skinflint like Rita. In spite of her own indignant protests that she'd earned the full $7.42 they'd agreed on, and that Rita should have hidden the spiral pad somewhere instead of just leaving it on her bed for Mrs. Rowan to find, the most Rita would hand over was half.

Angie scowled down at the gleaming dark expanse of Heron Lake, spangled with star reflections like tossed coins. She told herself that $3.71 wasn't really very much money at all. If she asked her mother for it and made up a reasonable fib about why she needed it, her mother would probably hand the money over without fuss. Sure, that was the thing to do—simple and easy. So why was she making such a big deal about it? In fact, she'd do it now, tonight, if she could catch her mother alone.

She turned to look at the lighted windows of the cabin and saw that the card game was breaking up. Her father was getting to his feet, yawning, while Steve gathered up the cards and shuffled them before putting them back in their box. The two of them were always trying to stack the deck on each other—sort of a joke, but not really. Angie had caught each of them trying to arrange the cards so that they looked okay but when reshuffled a couple of times would fall into a planned order. This seemed impossible to her, but then, they were the clever ones.

Angie sighed and pushed herself heavily to her feet. She thought of how her mother often stayed up reading in the living room after everyone else had gone to bed. That was when Angie would creep back in and make her pitch. Once she had the money, she'd lock it in the cashbox, put the key back in her empty wallet, and have a really good night's sleep for the first time since Courtney's letter had arrived.

That was what she was thinking as she crossed the porch, swung the screen door open, and nudged the inner door with her knee—it had a tendency to stick. But somehow it wasn't what she did. Instead, as the three faces turned toward her, she squared her shoulders, took a deep breath, and said loudly, "I need three dollars and seventy-one cents. I mean, I really *need* it."

Everyone looked startled. Angie was horrified at herself. She hadn't even thought up a fib yet.

"Well, now, I think we can probably manage that,"

her father said mildly, and added, "Close the door, Angie, you're letting in a lot of cold air. Three seventy-one, eh? As an advance on next month's allowance, I assume?" Angie nodded mutely. "A curious sum," he observed, and held up a hand. "No, no, don't explain— I'm sure there's a story behind it, but I think I'd just as soon not know what it is."

He chuckled. Angie's mother was already reaching for her purse. "Oh, Angie," she said with a sigh, "you're even worse about money than I was at your age. It used to run through my fingers like water. Three dollars and seventy-one cents, you said?"

Only Steve looked thoughtful. But even Steve couldn't have figured the whole thing out this fast, Angie thought a little wildly. It was much too complicated. Then his face cleared. "Backgammon with Sally, I bet," he said in an undertone—their father didn't like them to gamble. "She's getting pretty good, thanks to all the times I've beaten her."

Smirking, he stood up to return the cards and score pad to the shelf, then turned to help his father fold up the table.

Angie stared at her family, the three people she knew best in the world—her vigorous, impatient father, wearing an old Ragg sweater over his khaki pants; her graceful mother, in lemon-yellow warm-ups; her self-assured brother, in a loud plaid shirt and faded jeans. She wasn't even going to need a fib, she realized. They all just accepted that she had gotten herself into another minor, boring muddle—scatterbrained Angie, who couldn't be expected to function the way smarter, more organized people did.

"Here," Mrs. Hyatt said, holding out a hand. "Three seventy-five. I don't seem to have any pennies, but what's another four cents?"

Angie started to take the money, then pulled her hand back slowly. "No," she said, "you need to know what I did—*why* I need the money."

Her father was yawning again, wedging the card table against the wall behind the couch. "Can't it wait till morning, Angie? I'm beat—I got too much sun out on the Sailfish this afternoon."

"You went sailing?" Steve turned on him in outrage. "Why didn't you tell me? I wouldn't have gone on that boring old hike up Harriman Mountain if I'd known."

"Now, Steve—" his mother began.

"I need to tell you!" Angie said, stamping her foot. "It's important." Suddenly her knees felt weak. She sat down hard on the straight chair beside the stove, stared at the floor, and announced unhappily, "I'm a thief."

That got everyone's attention, though not quite in the way she'd intended. They all burst out laughing.

"I am," she insisted, raising her chin. "I stole money from the club treasury." When they looked blank, she said, "You know, my baton-twirling club."

"Oh, that," said Steve. "Well, *they'll* never miss it.

Talk about a bunch of ditsy girls—I bet they can't even count."

"They will too miss it," Angie said angrily. "They need it for uniforms. In fact they've already bought them, or Courtney's mother has—these blue, I mean green, satin shorts with a white stripe down the side."

That set Steve off again. Mrs. Hyatt said, "Oh, Angie, maybe you borrowed some money, but that's not the same thing as stealing."

"It is if you can't pay it back. I tried," Angie said with a sudden wail, "but I just couldn't get it all."

"Well, but if this is all you're missing . . ." Looking bewildered, her mother held out the money again—three dollar bills, three quarters.

"But I can't let you just *give* it to me! I thought I could, but I can't. It would be wrong."

"The video," Steve said suddenly.

Angie looked at him gratefully. Never in her wildest dreams could she have imagined being glad that Steve had ferreted out one of her secrets, but right now she welcomed him as an ally. "Right," she said. "And I thought I could put the money back when I got next month's allowance, but then Courtney's mother—"

"Courtney's mother again," Mr. Hyatt said heavily. He shook his head, sighed, and dumped some more wood in the stove. "Looks like it's going to be a long night," he muttered, pulling out a chair. "Okay, let's take it from the top—Courtney's mother or the video, whichever came first."

So they all sat down again while Angie poured out her story. She told about buying the video and sneaking it back to Potter's; about trying to earn money from tips; how she'd thought of borrowing from Rita but had wound up selling her the video instead. She told about Rita's hiring her to make up ideas for a story, and how that hadn't quite worked out either. Along the way, she also explained about Hugh Curtis and how he'd blackmailed her into giving him canoe lessons.

When she'd finished, she sat back, flushed with exertion and with the unaccustomed sensation of having her family listen to her for whole minutes at a time without interrupting.

Steve said wonderingly, "That Rita is some operator. Half price for the video, you said, and then half for the story ideas too? I mean, even if she didn't wind up using them . . ." He shook his head in admiration.

"Well, thank goodness," said Mrs. Hyatt. "It's just such a relief to know why you've seemed so different these last few days. Not flitting from one thing to another the way you usually do, but seeming so . . . well, *intense*, almost."

"Comparatively speaking, anyway," Steve murmured.

"Hugh Curtis in a canoe," Mr. Hyatt said, and gave a sudden roar of laughter. "Now that I'd like to have seen."

"You still can," Angie said. "I owe him two more lessons." She frowned at her family. She knew she ought to feel relieved by their attitude, but somehow— "Aren't you *mad*?" she asked.

Her father shrugged. "Well, I'm not too happy about your sneaking that video home with you, but it looks as if that's Rita's problem now—or Rita's family's problem, anyway. Giant leeches, did you say?"

"In French," Steve put in.

"Really, Angie," said her mother.

They were all laughing again.

"But—but what about stealing and lying?" Angie demanded. Suddenly she was furious at her parents, and maybe at herself, too. "If it was Steve instead of me, you wouldn't be laughing. If Steve did something sneaky and dishonest, you'd punish him. Well, wouldn't you?"

"Hey, don't drag me into your sordid little adventures," Steve said. His parents ignored him, looking thoughtful.

"Maybe so," Mr. Hyatt said. He studied Angie for a long moment, his brow creased as if he'd never really looked at her before. "Is that what you want, Angie—to be punished?"

Angie thought about it. "Well, I guess I don't *want* to be," she allowed. "That would be kind of sick. I guess it's more wanting to be taken—well, seriously. You know, instead of just having everyone go 'Oh, Angie' whenever I mess up."

Her father nodded slowly. Angie's mother made a wry face and said, "I know the feeling." She opened her hand, in which she still held the three dollar bills and the three quarters. "Well, now, what about this?"

When Angie hesitated, Mr. Hyatt observed, "Seems to me Angie's already done a pretty good job of punishing herself. Lord knows she's worked hard enough." He chuckled again, smoothed his face out hastily, and said to Angie, "My vote goes for putting this money straight in the cashbox and deducting it from your September allowance. What do you say?"

Angie still hesitated, strongly tempted. Then she shook her head. "I guess I'd feel better if I earned it," she said with a sigh.

Steve groaned. "Boy, Angie, you don't know a good deal when you see one."

Their father said, "Well, I think that could be arranged. We must have a chore or two around here that needs doing." He considered a moment. "The front porch could use a good sweeping."

"And I'd love it if someone would put the tennis rackets back in their cases," Mrs. Hyatt said. "And collect all the balls, too, and get rid of the dead ones. Golf balls, too—they're all over the place."

Angie frowned. "It can't be something dumb like that," she said. "It's gotta be something *hard*, that I'll really hate doing."

"I know," Steve said gleefully. "The laundry."

Trust Steve. Usually their parents took turns doing Laundromat duty in Gilead while everyone else went off to stroll around and play video games and have ice-cream cones. Angie listened stoically while it was agreed that this job would fall to her on Monday morning. She would have to remember to put the soap in, to transfer the wet clothes to a drier as soon as one was free, and to fold them before the wrinkles set.

"And make sure you have the right change to begin with," her mother reminded her as they all stood up and Mr. Hyatt banked the stove for the night. "That's always such a nuisance." She paused. "Of course, there's probably plenty of change in your cashbox. . . ."

"No," Angie said, clutching the precious $3.75 she'd finally accepted. "Once this money is in there, I'm never opening that box again. In fact, I'm never going to be treasurer again." She thought for a moment. "I think I'll run for vice president instead."

* * *

As she and Steve stood waiting their turn for the bathroom, Steve said, "Hey, I just thought of something. You don't have to give Hugh Curtis any more canoe lessons, now that you've spilled all the beans."

Angie started to smile, then bit her lip, reconsidering. "I promised him, though."

"Well, hey, that was blackmail." Steve shrugged. "Besides, people are always promising Hugh things, just to get rid of him. He's used to it."

Angie thought that was probably true. She also thought that with two more lessons, Hugh might possibly be able to handle a bow paddle, as long as someone who knew what she was doing took charge of the stern.

"I'll think about it," she said.

Don't Get Mad, Get Even!

by Rona S. Zable

Watch out for Megan Dooley! Her motto is "Don't get mad, get even"—and she's already scared away six housekeepers. Even Megan's next-door neighbors, Bart Peckham and his stuck-up sister, Vonna Mae, aren't safe from Megan's pranks.

Then Housekeeper #7 shows up. Daphne Winston has to be the worst housekeeper in the world, but she *is* full of surprises. As Megan plans her best trick yet on Bart Peckham, Daphne teaches her an unexpected lesson—the best revenge of all!

0-8167-3574-3 $2.95 U.S./$3.95 Can.

Available wherever you buy books.